A
Novel
Written By
D.C. MARSHALL

WHEN THE DEVIL LAUGHS

BOOK ONE

ISBN 13: 978-0-9918913-0-6 [eBook]
ISBN 13: 978-0-9918913-1-3 [Print]
ISBN-10: 0991891317 [Print]

Edition 4
Final Revision

When The Devil Laughs – Book One – (edition 4) Final Revision
Copyright © 2013 D.C. Marshall All Rights Are Reserved.
ISBN 13: 978-0-9918913-1-3 (Print)
ISBN 10: 0991891317 (Print)
ISBN 13: 978-0-9918913-0-6 [eBook]
BISAC: Fiction / Suspense
Written by, D.C. Marshall
Edited by, D.C. Marshall
Published by, D.C. Marshall April, 2013 D.C. Marshall
Printed May, 2013 - Paper Back 6x9
Interior Page Count –217 Pages – Includes Intro to When Angels Smile (Book Two)
When The Devil Laughs – Book One – (edition 4) Cover Final Revision
Copyright © 2013 D.C. Marshall All Rights Are Reserved.
Cover Designed by, D.C. Marshall Copyright © 2013 D.C. Marshall
When The Devil Laughs – Book One – (edition 4) [eBook] April, 2013
When The Devil Laughs – Book One – (edition 4) PRINT May, 2013

Table of Contents

To all of my family and to Gailene, without your love and patience, I would never have been able to finish what I started.

"The Devil only laughs when he is free!"

Chapter 1

Tonya Wells-Marx

April 22nd, 2010. 6:00 pm

Tonya Wells-Marx had just arrived in Playa Del Carmen (PDC), after flying into Cancun from the JFK International Airport in New York. Her mother, Sandra picked her up at the Cancun airport and drove them back to her small one bedroom flat in PDC.

They had not seen each other for almost a year; since Tonya had been completing her final year of studies at Pratt University, in Brooklyn, New York. She graduated with honors. As a reward to herself she thought she'd take a little holiday, spend some time in the sun, and God willing spend a couple days catching up with her mother.

When they arrived at Sandra's flat about 45 minutes later, they did end up spending a few hours catching up. Tonya reminisced about her school year and about a guy she had been dating but recently broke up with. His name was Tom. He too was a fashion student.

"He was just too flaky for me mom. And I seriously think he was confused with his sexuality" Tonya explained.

Sandra smirked "Well he was in fashion…" She said with a chuckle. They both had a good laugh at that.

Sandra was delighted to see that her daughter; after listening to her for the past three hours; seemed to have grown up so much this past year.

Tonya seemed serious about her career in fashion, and it sounded like she was well on her way to achieving some success, as Tonya had also confided to her that she landed a job as an intern junior assistant fashion designer for Gucci starting in June.

Sandra realized that Tonya was probably at a point in her life where maturity and security were important to her and came to her own conclusion that Tonya was probably looking to find a man who was mature and stable in a career, rather than some college boy with his head still in the clouds, and confused about his own sexuality.

Sandra was meeting with a man tomorrow morning who fit that bill perfectly. She was going to be showing him a beach-front investment property. This man was in his early 30's and he was rich and successful. He was also very good looking (or so Sandra thought in her opinion.) He might have been a good prospect for Tonya. Sandra started thinking it might not be such a bad idea to introduce the two of them to each other.

"Speaking of which… I have a meeting with a charming young man tomorrow." Sandra spoke up with a suggestive tone.

"Oh gosh no, do me a favor mom and don't try and set me up with anyone, Please!" Tonya moaned. That was the last thing that she wanted.

"No wait, listen. He's a very successful young man. He purchased a villa on Cozumel through me a couple years ago and made a ton of money, and now he's looking to buy some investment property here in Playa Del Carmen." Sandra tried making her case to her daughter.

"Mom, please." Tonya moaned and rolled her eyes. "I don't need or want to be set up on a date with anyone."

"Who said anything about a date?" Sandra interrupted.

"I'm just saying I'm meeting him tomorrow, maybe you should come along, and you can see for yourself." Sandra paused for a second. "And did I mention that he was handsome?"

"You said he was charming." Tonya mumbled.

Sandra smiled. "Very charming, successful, handsome, and rich!" she said emphasizing all of his wonderful traits. Sandra paused for a minute looking at her daughter. "All you have to do is come with me, and see for yourself Tonya — come on you have nothing to lose, and nothing else better to do tomorrow anyways."

"Well I don't know. I'll see how I feel tomorrow." Tonya murmured submitting a little to the idea.

"Good. At least think about it. You never know how things might turn out."

"We'll see mom." Tonya said covering a yawn that had been aching to get out. She was getting tired. She might have had a little jet leg or maybe it was just the fact that she had been up since 4am, and had a busy day.

Either way she was ready to crash for the night.

ooooo

—

Chapter 2

Luke Cassalon

Luke Cassalon was a wealthy 33 year old American man who was living on a yacht that he named The Monster's Ball — living and sailing between the Gulf of Mexico and the Caribbean Sea for the past five years. He spent the last five years basking in the tropics — making short visits to every major, city port between Miami and Panama.

Luke graduated from Harvard with a master's degree in Computer Science at the age of 25. He didn't make his multi-million dollar fortune by working for any hi-tech corporations or social media sites. He was much too independent and non-conforming for that.

Instead Luke made his fortune by tapping into the world wide web of pornography; only the kind of pornography that Luke Cassalon provided access to was the kind of pornography that was, black market, amateur voyeur, snuff. It was the kind of stuff that only the sickest and most twisted perverts would find pleasure in viewing.

They paid big money to watch it.

Business was good for Luke. The fact that he was a multi millionaire was proof of that but it was haunting to think that it also meant that there were so many demented people in the world who actually paid to watch the filth that he sold.

The pornography he sold involved young, college aged women between the ages 18 to 25 who were both drunk and drugged and taken advantage of once they passed out.

This kind of pornography never had a happy ending.

Luke was in the prime of his life and was enjoying every dark moment of it. He was well aware that he would probably go straight to hell — *if there was a hell* — for all the pain and suffering done to these young women; and because he profited from their pain and misery, and deaths. Yet he had no plans to repent or to change his life in any way. He regretted nothing. He had all the money and all the freedom in the world to do as he pleased. He would take what he wanted when he wanted, and give nothing back. He felt he was above everything and everyone else. He felt as though the world was his playground, and it was his to enjoy.

Luke had completely lost track of what was right and what was wrong, and the dark void inside of him was growing so large and so quickly because of all of the unforgivable and immoral things he had surrounded his life with, that he had become twisted and actually felt himself becoming soulless.

He was empty inside and found himself to be always searching for something else to fill that deep, hungry void with.

Luke was never able to satisfy his insatiable need for more, no matter how much he tried and no matter how much he fed into it, nothing could fill it. He was beyond all hope and there was no turning back for him.

The only way to go — *was forward*-and forward for Luke meant taking a deeper journey into the dark madness of his existence.

ooooo

Chapter 3

The Monster's Ball

April 23rd, 2010. 10:30 am CST.

The yacht named The Monster's Ball sailed up to one of the public docks in Playa Del Carmen, Mexico. Luke had plans for the day. He was first going to check into a resort named the Grand Portos Resort (GPR), before meeting up with a real estate broker named Sandra to view a multi million dollar beachfront property.

Luke's friend, room mate, and business partner Jacob Stanley was staying behind on the yacht. Someone needed to stay behind and protect it. There was too much cash and valuables aboard to trust leaving it unattended at a public dock.

The Monster's Ball was a multi million dollar, luxury sport yacht. It was a limited edition C&B special, with a custom designed interior. It was powered by two diesel Volvo D13 800 hp engines. Only 3 models of these yachts existed. It had an enclosed cockpit and helm with a 360 degree panoramic view. Below the cockpit, was the bridge that had a hot tub and outside grill with a horseshoe shaped, white leather sofa.

Inside the yacht were all the bells and whistles, stainless steel appliances, granite countertops, marble flooring and 3 bedrooms. In total the yacht was 17 meters long from nose to motor, 7 meters wide, and 15 meters high from keel to top. It was painted white on the exterior with a blue accent gel coat wrapping around the hull.

It was one of those showpieces that demanded your attention, and your first thought would be that whoever owned it was wealthier than most people could ever hope to be.

"I've got some business to take care of, so meet me back here — say at about 6:00pm." Luke said.
Jacob just gave a nod as he released the anchor and started tossing the cleat ropes over the side of the yacht and said,

"Yah sure buddy, I'll be here. Do you wanna just tie the ropes off on the dock posts before you go?"

Luke climbed down the ladder on the side of the yacht and jumped onto the dock. He tied off the yacht and walked away without saying another word to Jacob. He walked straight down the crowded beaches and was headed for the Grand Portos Resort (GPR).

ooooo

Chapter 4

Jacob Stanley

Jacob Stanley was 32 years old. He first met Luke in Miami Florida, at a beach party. Unlike Luke he had no university degree, and had little or no knowledge of computers let alone the understanding of how to design a website and administrate it on the internet.

The extent of Jacob's knowledge in computers was how to login to his email provider, compose an email, and send it.

Jacob was however an Ex-Navy SEAL. He became a SEAL when he was just 22 years old. He served a 1 year tour in Iraq, and 2 years in Afghanistan. By the time he was 25 he disappeared off the grid. He was presumed dead by the military after he was sent into the Kashmir's to stir things up a bit.

Jacob did a good job of that, and he liked to blow shit up!

Jacob created tensions between the Taliban, the Pakistani's, and the Indian's. He and his small crew of SEALS would level whole villages, and create mayhem. They would leave behind false evidence, so that one of the forces would suspect and blame the other, so it created a vicious circle of revenge and hate between them.

Jacob's crew was called 'D-Company' and they were one of the darkest, dirtiest, and deadliest group of Black Ops SEALS the US ever trained. Jacob's 'D-Company' of course never existed according to the pentagon.

By the time he was 25 Jacob had seen and done so many horrific things that he lost touch with humanity. He was sociopathic–detached from guilt or conscience, and incapable of knowing right from wrong. He was deranged and because of his skills, training, and hands on experience of being a living, breathing, psychopathic soldier – he turned into a sick and twisted monster.

The only pleasure Jacob felt, was when he inflicted pain onto others. The more innocent – the greater the rush he got from it. He liked his victims being helpless yet aware. He liked feeling that sense of control over them. As such; he was the one who raped the hundreds of drunk and drugged young women on camera, and took their lives in the end. He let Luke handle the business end of it and sell it to the perverts who were eagerly willing to pay to watch it.

When Jacob went (AWOL) and disappeared off the grid, he surfaced in china and the first thing he did was hitch a ride back to North America on a cargo ship that happened to be illegally smuggling refugees into Western Canada. He got off the ship in Vancouver but many young female, Chinese refugees weren't so lucky. Jacob cut their voyage and lives – short.

Once in Canada Jacob quickly made his way down to the border between the province of British Columbia and Washington State. He easily slipped past border patrol by crossing over into Washington State through some un-patrolled farm in the late hours of night.

Jacob took his time as he traveled across the country, leaving behind a string of unsolved crimes; home invasions, robberies, rapes, arson, even murders. He continued his violent crime spree south-east across the country until he arrived in Miami, Florida.

One night Jacob stumbled upon a beach party and that's where and when he first met Luke. Jacob never expected to become friends with anyone – ever; let alone with someone as unlikely a match to him as Luke Cassalon was.

It was hard to say what it was exactly that made him even listen to Luke, except for maybe that he actually believed Luke when he had told him that he could make millions of dollars by uploading sex video's to the web, the more twisted and dirtier — the better.

Jacob took a chance and made a deal with Luke. He told Luke that he would record something so sick and twisted that it would blow his mind. That's how it all started. From that moment on — they clicked. They were partners in crime, and like Luke had said; they were soon millionaires.

The recordings didn't end...

The demand kept growing and so did the supply but the danger of being caught became riskier as well.

They decided they needed to be mobile. That's when they bought The Monster's Ball and began to sail the gulf, and the Caribbean.

5 years later, they obviously never stopped and never looked back.

ooooo

Chapter 5

Tonya gets ready

April 23rd, 2010. 9:00 am CST.

"Come on we're going to be late and I can't be late!" Sandra was in a panic. She woke up late. She forgot to set her alarm, and she had to meet Luke Cassalon.

Tonya pulled herself up. Her legs dangled over the sofa that she slept on. She sat up, still wrapped in the warm afghan her mother had knit for her back when Tonya was just 12 years old. She had not felt the warm wool around her since she first left home back 4 years ago when she left for University. It brought back a familiar feeling of being young and innocent.

She felt like a teenager again.

"Come on Tonya, go hop in the shower and get ready!" Sandra barked as she rifled through papers that were strewn about all over the kitchen table.

Tonya yawned and stretched her arms. Slowly she stood up from the sofa. "I'm not even sure I want to go mom." She murmured still feeling half asleep.

"Nonsense, you'll feel better after you hop in the shower." Sandra persisted.

Tonya sighed, she really didn't feel like meeting anyone today, but after standing up from the sofa and feeling the warm rays of the Mexican sun beating down on her face through the living room window, she couldn't resist the urge to wake up and get out of the small, stuffy, little loft. She slowly made her way to the washroom and stepped into the shower after stripping from her pajama shorts and tank top.

She was in the shower a good fifteen minutes before she stepped back out and wrapped her-self up in towels and started getting ready.

Tonya started by carefully moisturizing her body from neck to toe with some shimmering body lotion. *It made her skin sparkle and feel like silk.* Then she blow dried her hair. Next was her makeup. She penciled around her eye lids with a black eye crayon. *It made her green eyes beam like emeralds.* Then she carefully applied her foundation and a bit of teal eye shadow. Next; she carefully tweezed her eyebrows into a thin slightly curved line. *It made her look demure but pensive at the same time.* The final touch to her makeup was brushing her lashes with an eyelash extension brush, and applying a rose tinted lip gloss to her bow-shaped lips.

When Tonya was done applying her makeup she used a flat iron to straighten her long, white blond hair — she pulled her bangs back from her forehead using a pearl beaded head band. It made her hair look like a golden veil of satin as it arched and hung loosely around her beautiful, oval shaped face.

Finally Tonya was ready to get dressed. She slipped into a white and pink trimmed Victoria Secret thong and matching push up bra. 'She wanted her 34b's to look like 34c's today.' She pulled out a one piece, sheer silky chiffon, cream, colored sundress, and a wide satin, brown sash that she would use to tie around her thin 24 inch waist. She finished off her outfit by slipping on a pair of white 5 inch heels.

Sandra marveled at how beautiful her daughter looked, as she walked out of the washroom, and she loved the dress she was wearing.

"Oh my god Tonya, you look amazing!" she complimented her, "…and that dress is spectacular." She continued feeling the silky chiffon it was made from.
Tonya smiled. "Thanks." She paused for a second modeling it for her mother, turning from front, to side, to back, then back to face her again.

"I made it you know?"

"Are you serious?" Sandra gasped. She almost didn't believe Tonya but clearly her daughter had an eye for fashion.

Sandra just stared at her for a long minute in silence. She felt proud and happy for her daughter that she could make herself up to look so good, like a fashion model. She only wished she still had that ability to look so good. Sandra suddenly felt a little envious of her daughter. She couldn't compete with her now.

Sandra felt old and weathered in comparison.

By 10:30am they were both dressed, and ready to go. They left Sandra's loft and were soon on their way driving in Sandra's black SUV to the Grand Portos Resort (GPR) to meet with Luke Cassalon.

∞∞∞∞∞

Chapter 6

Brock, Quinn, and Maria arrive in PDC

April 23rd, 2010. 10:30 am CST.

Brock Castegere, Quinn Bailey, and Maria Carter arrived in Playa Del Carmen, Mexico. They flew in from a privately owned air strip in New York, on a small Honda HA-420 prototype business jet. It was a small private jet that was designed to hold 1 to 2 crew members, and 5 passengers. It was no more than 42 ft long, and had a wingspan of 39 ft wide. It was equipped with two GE Honda HF120 turbo fan engines and could reach a maximum speed of 483 miles per hour. It took just over 4 hours to arrive.

They made great time!

Brock Castegere was the 27 year old heir to a multi billion dollar estate left to him by his father Henry Castegere; co-founder of C&B Inc. His father; Henry passed away suddenly in his sleep in January of 2006, from a massive myocardial infarction (a heart attack) at the age of 62. Five years before Henry's death, Brock lost his mother, to cancer.

Quinn Bailey was also 27 years old and also an heir to the multi-billion dollar estate left to him by his parents Brian and Shannon Bailey. Brian was Henry's business partner who was the other co-founder of C&B Inc.

19

However unlike Brock, Quinn's parents died when he was only 5 years old, in a terrible head on collision with a tractor trailer in the Rocky Mountain passes of Colorado. Subsequent to his parent's deaths, Quinn was adopted and raised by Henry and Theresa. It wasn't hard to understand that Brock and Quinn were in every sense of the word — brothers.

Maria Carter was Brock's 24 year old cousin. She was the daughter of Henry's younger sister Martha who was married to Phil Carter. Strangely enough she was also the love of Quinn Bailey's life, and he was the love of hers. Their affections for each other began at an early age, and it was as evident as it was inevitable, that they would some day be together — wedded in holy matrimony.

It was only a matter of time!

When they landed and came to a full stop they exited the jet and walked down the steps onto the tarmac of the small airfield. They breathed in the hot sultry air, and felt the sun's deep warming rays melt into their skin immediately. They felt refreshed, revived, and glad to be there. They were in the heart of the Mexican Riviera and it felt like paradise compared to the cool spring weather that they just left behind in Manhattan.

A limousine was parked just off to the side of the tarmac waiting for them. A chauffeur stood in front of the driver's side door. He looked hot and overdressed in the black suit and tie, he was wearing. He stood with his legs wide apart and his hands clutched together in front of him. He was a short man, Hispanic, and in his mid forties. At first glance he looked like Joe Pesci out of the movie Goodfella's. Bill Creston the pilot stepped out of the jet behind Brock, Quinn and Maria.

"Well enjoy your stay!" Bill said as he reached out his hand toward the three of them.

"Will do Bill. And thanks again. You got us here in record time!" Brock replied as he shook Bill's hand.

"That's why you pay me the big bucks, Brock." Bill replied with a wink. "Anyways, go have your fun in the sun, and take care huh! I'll see you all in a week from now."

The trio walked toward the chauffeur and the limousine. They each carried one piece of luggage. Brock and Quinn had duffle bags, while Maria pulled a large hard-top suitcase on rollers behind her.

The chauffeur smiled and greeted them with "Hola!" before he quickly opened the doors to the back of the limousine for them. He took their bags and packed them into the trunk as they climbed inside. He shut their doors when he finished packing their luggage into the trunk and quickly climbed into the driver's seat.

He turned the key and the engine turned over with a quiet hum. A tinted window behind his seat separating the front of the limousine from the back of it, slid down quietly and smoothly.

"Welcome to Playa Del Carmen. I'm your chauffeur, Miguel Sanchez and I'll be driving you to your destination."

"Thank you Miguel." Maria said with a smile.

"If there is anything you need, anything at all, just let me know" Miguel continued. He spoke fast and had a noticeable Mexican accent but he spoke English very well and he was easy to understand.

"Yah thanks Miguel. We'll let you know for sure, if we need anything." Quinn added as he fished around inside the mini bar. He found three champagne glasses and a bottle of champagne packed in ice.

"You know where we're heading right Miguel?" Brock asked just to make sure.

"Yes señor" Miguel answered with a nod then shifted the limousine into drive "To the GPR, señor."

"GPR?" Brock asked with a slightly confused look on his face.

"GRAND.PORTOS.RESORT." Quinn interrupted saying each word with a slow pause in between.
Brock shook his head "Oh yah of course." He felt a little stupid that he didn't catch that!
Maria just laughed.

Quinn popped the cork from the champagne bottle, it fizzed and some of it bubbled out of the neck of the bottle. He began to pour them each a drink. He handed Brock and Maria their glass one by one and then poured himself one. A moment later he lifted his glass in the air ready to make a toast.

"Here's to being in paradise." Luke toasted.
"Cheers!" Brock toasted.
"To paradise" Maria added.

They touched each others champagne glasses and took a drink. The window behind Miguel began to slide back up.

None of them even noticed!

Maria couldn't resist as she watched Brock and Quinn take such small sips from their champagne glasses — she had already drained her glass empty.

She set her glass down beside her and suddenly lifted her hands to tip both their glasses up so it overflowed in their mouths and raced down their throats. They both looked stunned for just a split second. Brock spat champagne everywhere and choked. While Quinn just sat there letting the champagne drool down his whiskery chin onto his lap.

"You are going to pay for that dearly tonight, my love." He murmured as a wolfish smile had spread across his face. He blinked slowly with his gaze locked hungrily on Maria.

"Oh is that a promise?" Maria asked with a laugh.
"You better believe it is." Quinn assured her then leaned forward to melt his lips against hers.

Brock wiped the champagne he spat up off his face and leaned over to take the bottle from Quinn with a sigh, as the two love birds were lip-locked. He took a big swig straight from the bottle then raised it over their heads and let it pour over them. The party started!

About 20 minutes later…

Miguel Sanchez pulled the limousine into a vacant parking spot behind a black SUV that was parked right outside of the GPR. The window behind his seat slid down quietly again.

"We have arrived!" he announced to the trio in the back of his limousine.

"Wow that was fast Miguel!" They all shouted as one. It seemed like a very short ride. Minutes at most, but was actually closer to a 20 minute drive from the time that they left the small runway where their jet had landed.

They were so busy laughing it made the time race by. Maria's hair was still damp from the champagne Brock had poured over their heads earlier, and Quinn was wearing only his boxer briefs. They had been poking fun at how some men; especially the European kind wore those skimpy little Speedo swimsuits (*or banana hammocks as some call them*) at the beach parading around their packages. They had also dared Quinn to walk into the lobby of the GPR wearing just his boxer briefs—*and now*-the moment of truth.

Miguel stepped out of the limousine and went to the trunk to remove their luggage before opening the doors for them.   They filed out one by one. Brock was first, then Maria, and finally Quinn. Brock and Maria stood beside Miguel and watched as Quinn emerged from the Limousine.

Quinn was apprehensive at first. He was nervous and shy for just a split second before he must have remembered he was actually a good looking buffed young man. He had round muscles and stood 6ft tall. He had shaggy long blonde hair; it was the surfer dude look. His chest was thick and broad. He lifted weights 3 days a week and kept to a good nutritional diet so he had a nice tone, and the 6 pack abs to show off. Suddenly he didn't feel intimated at all as he stepped out of the limousine. He was quite confident that his package bulged large enough to measure up to any man who might be parading around in a banana hammock. He stood straight and tall puffing out his chest a little as if he were proud to display himself.

Brock and Maria laughed hysterically, especially when Miguel blinked rapidly with a puzzled look on his face as Quinn stood before him in only his briefs. Quinn kept a stoic look on his face as he reached down and grabbed his duffle bag. He slung it over his shoulder.

"Well shall we check in ladies and Gentlemen?" Quinn said as he winked to Maria.

"You bet!" Brock said and reached into his pocket. He pulled out a fold of money. He pinched four crisp hundred dollar bills between his fingers and pulled them free. He handed them to Miguel and reached out to shake his hand.

"Thanks so much Miguel."

Miguel shook Brock's hand and nodded, glancing at the 4 one hundred dollar bills. A smile spread across his face and he said "Gracia's and thank you so much senor"

Miguel looked at all three of them. They looked like such an attractive bunch. Especially Maria — *she was so sweet and pretty* — he couldn't resist. He had to take a picture. Miguel pulled out his phone thumbed the camera button and lifted it up.

"Smile for me." He said and snapped a picture of the three of them.

They all looked a little surprised but laughed it off, thinking maybe he took pictures of everyone that he drove.

24

Miguel smiled and slipped his phone back into his pocket quickly.

"Thanks Miguel, I'm sure we'll be calling you in a few days." Maria said as she hooked her arm around Quinn's. She had already slipped Miguel's business card she had grabbed from the back of the limousine into a side pocket of her black leather Gucci purse.

Quinn and Maria felt a lot of eyes staring at them as they proceeded inside the lobby of the GPR. Whether people were actually staring at them was questionable but it certainly felt like it to them.

Brock was following close behind them with a smirk on his face. He couldn't help but feel bemused watching them walk into the crowded lobby as proud and as in love as two people could be.

Maria looked as adorable as ever.

The youthful bounce in her step matched with her petite thin little figure made her seem so sweet and vibrant. She was all of 5 ft 1 and weighed no more than a hundred pounds.

Maria was wearing a thin cotton floral, pattern sun dress that had spaghetti straps draped over her tiny shoulders. The dress clung to her small curves perfectly, and it stopped just short of her knees. She was wearing 4 inch black leather gladiator heels that had criss-crossed straps that circled around her ankles to just below her calves.

Maria's hair was caramel brown in color, and it hung stylishly midway down her back. She had a sparkling butterfly clip adorned with diamonds clipped to one side of her head. It pinned her hair back tightly on one side, leaving a thick strand of long bangs hugging the other side of her face. Her skin had a nice shimmering gold tan, and it glittered as the sun rays bounced off her shoulders.

Maria glanced back at Brock and smiled as they walked toward the check-in counter. *Her complexion was flawless.* She had pouty shaped lips that were painted with candy apple red lipstick, which at the moment made her smile seem as bright as the sun. Her teeth were perfectly straight and glowing white. Her eyes were deep blue, similar to Brock's but not quite as deep, and they were wide with excitement. *A spark was dancing inside of them.* It wasn't hard to tell that she and Brock were related. She was often mistaken for his younger sister when they were seen together.

Brock himself had deep warm blue eyes — though his hair was raven black; which he inherited from his mother's side. It was long and wavy but done in a stylish fashion where it hung just to his shoulders. He had roughly the same build as Quinn. They worked out together and kept to the same nutritional diet, so beneath his white short sleeve button up shirt he had the muscles and abs too. He wore some baggy cargo shorts and a set of sandals. His legs were strong and thick looking. He had the whole package. He was good looking and knew it. His face had been on the cover of GQ a few times as he posed for them on some of the luxury yachts his company C&B Inc. designed and were marketing.

Brock was the poster boy for C&B Inc!

Quinn's look was a little different. He looked like a surfer dude, or an adrenalin junky. He sported a little moustache and goatee; he looked rough around the edges and a little more hardened. Quinn was fair haired and his eyes were a brighter blue. Quinn and Brock looked similar but opposite in so many ways.

Just before they reached the check in counter they walked past a young woman that caught Brock's eye.

She forced Brock's head to turn and follow her as she walked passed him. She was heading outside through the lobby. She was beautiful and looked like she was glowing in a halo of light. Brock was awestruck, and not just from her gorgeous face but by the way she walked past him like she was a runway model with her hips grinding shamelessly.

The sight of her stopped Brock in his tracks.

Brock just stared and watched her as she walked outside. She glanced back at him, and shot him a sexy smile before getting into the back of the black SUV that was parked outside.

∞∞∞∞

Chapter 7

Tonya meets Luke

April 23, 2010. 11:00 am CST.

Luke rented a room at the GPR. He was to meet Sandra at 11:00 am, so he had managed his time perfectly. He was given a complimentary glass of champagne when he checked in and started to sip on that while he waited for Sandra to show. Luke glanced to the Rolex on his wrist.

It was 11:00 am exactly.

Sandra sauntered into the lobby at that precise second — just as Luke looked back up from his watch. He recognized her immediately — he had met her before, after all. Her distinctive long blond hair gave her away instantly. Her hair was straight and flat, and fell down past her waist.

Sandra wasn't someone who you'd not notice.

Sandra was a tall woman approximately 5ft 10 barefoot. With heels on, she stood well over six feet tall. Luke had honestly thought Sandra wasn't half bad looking for a woman in her 50's, she looked more like a woman in her late 30's when he had first met her two years ago.

Even now, Sandra was in great shape, she had a great smile, and a fantastic pair of legs. She wasn't his type though—not by a long shot. He wasn't attracted to women older than himself for one thing, and she was much too headstrong for his liking. She was all about the business which he didn't mind but something about her just reminded him of his own mother. What few memories he had left of his mother anyways.

His relationship with Sandra was strictly-business. She really fought hard for him when she landed him a great deal when he purchased the villa on Cozumel. She earned his respect and trust, having saved him several hundred thousand dollars. The asking price was 1.7 million. When all was said and done he purchased it for 1.4 million. A year later he sold it for 2.6 million.

It turned out to be a great investment for Luke.

Luke's eyes wandered helplessly over to the young woman who walked closely beside Sandra. The young woman looked like she was glowing as the sunlight radiated through the lobby like a heavenly backlight behind her. They walked close together, and though they were still maybe ten yards away from him, he quickly surmised that she must have been Sandra's daughter.

As they approached him—stopping just a step or two in front of him, there was no mistaking that they were most definitely mother and daughter. Their hair was similar in color, their skin tone as well, but more distinct than anything else, was the emerald green color of their eyes.

"Hello Mr. Cassalon. How are you?" Sandra greeted him and extended her hand to him.

Luke shook her hand and responded, "Doing good Sandra, how about you?"

Luke's eyes couldn't help but stray over to her daughter. Sandra noticed it quite obviously, and wasted no time in introducing them.

"Mr. Cassalon this is my daughter Tonya — Tonya this is Mr. Luke Cassalon."

"A pleasure." He said reaching out his hand to hers.

"Likewise!" she responded and allowed a small demure smile to form across her mouth.

"I hope you don't mind that Tonya will be joining us today?" Sandra interrupted. She could tell that Luke was taken with her daughter already. *What man wouldn't be?*

"No not at all." He replied and glanced back to Sandra. He didn't mind having the opportunity to get to know this beautiful young woman.

Luke's mind had already begun to fill with all sorts of naughty visions and thoughts.

Tonya studied Luke for a quick minute. The first thing she noticed about him was his narrow chiseled face, and his icy blue eyes. He had a lean build, and short, dark, spiky hair, *'a runner'* she thought.

Luke was wearing a simple white, polo shirt, with some baggy blue cargo shorts, and flip flop sandals. He was sporting some stubble, maybe three days worth of growth, it was hard to say but it wasn't thick. His voice was stern and strong sounding — and he definitely spent a lot of time in the sun, as he had a dark, rich Caribbean tan. When he shook her hand it felt firm and not so gentle. He wasn't half bad looking, but there was something about him that made her felt slightly uneasy. She couldn't quite put her finger on it, but it was almost as if she could sense that he had an aggressive nature about him.

"Well time is ticking. Should we go and see the property?" Sandra asked.

"Absolutely" Luke replied and followed behind the two of them as they turned around to walk back across the lobby again.

He enjoyed the view walking behind Tonya. She had a perfectly shaped derrière. It looked firm and round and she had an amazing walk that complimented it all the more. Her hips grinded alluringly — her legs extended straight and tight as she lead each step with her toe pointed downward. Her calf muscles looked taut and sexy and she had an insatiable walk that kept his eyes fixed on her.

Tonya could almost feel Luke's eyes staring at her ass but she was used to that. She often caught men just staring at it. She was just about to glance over her shoulder to catch him in the act, when something distracted her.

There in front of her was this guy (Quinn) walking into the lobby wearing only his black boxer briefs and beside him was a gorgeous, petite, young woman (Maria) who looked about the same age as her, maybe even younger, and she had her arm hooked through his. They were laughing so it was obviously some sort of inside joke.

Tonya tried not to look at the bulge of his package but couldn't help it. He had a great build and the washboard abs to match it. *'Nice!'* She thought to herself and then glanced back up.

Behind the laughing couple was a very handsome guy (Brock) with his long wavy black hair that stopped at his shoulders. His eyes were the deepest blue eyes she had ever seen. His face was chiseled, refined, but strong looking. He was very handsome — and they made eye contact. It was one of those moments that seemed to last forever and she felt an immediate connection to him.

It might have been love at first sight; that people often talk about, or maybe it was just two people who simply found each to be *HOT!* Whatever the case might have been, she couldn't help but to look over shoulder at him before she walked back outside.

31

She was very pleased to see he had stopped, and had turned around and was still looking at her. She gave him a sexy smile before getting into her mothers SUV.

∞∞∞∞∞

Chapter 8

Quinn Proposes

April 23rd, 2010. 5:00 pm CST.

Brock, Quinn, and Maria had spent most of the day tanning on the white, sandy beach drinking margaritas and coronas. They decided to return to their rooms, and get ready to go downtown to find a cozy little restaurant and have dinner. Brock didn't realize it but he must have had too much sun. He felt a little nauseous and dizzy as they made their way back to their side by side rooms.

Quinn and Maria shared a room together, while Brock had his own right beside them. They thought it was best that way because it was after all a vacation retreat. Neither Quinn nor Maria had any intention of being quiet during their 'alone' time at night.

"Listen you two go on ahead and have a nice dinner. I'm going to just catch a few winks — I think I had a little too much sun." Brock said sounding exasperated as he opened the door to his room.

"Are you sure?" Maria asked, with a concerned look on her face.

"Come on are you serious? It's our first night here man!" Quinn sighed in disappointment.

"Yeah — I'm sure. I just need a little rest before the night really starts — you know?"

Quinn just shrugged his shoulders and sighed, "Whatever!" He said before he went inside his and Maria's room.

Maria walked up to Brock and placed her hand on his forehead. She softly slid it down to his cheek and said, "You do feel a little hot."

Brock nodded and forced a small grin up one side of his mouth and murmured, "Yeah I know. I'll be ok though — I'm just tired. If I wake up before you guys get back, I'll be downstairs in the buffet room eating ok — we'll have some fun just the three of us later, I promise."

Maria smiled and stood on her tip toes and placed a soft kiss on Brock's cheek. "Ok — you rest up. We're going to have some fun tonight whether you're feeling better or not though — got that?"

"Got it" Brock chuckled and gave her a wink. "Now go on and have a nice dinner." He said as he started to shut his door.

"I will" Maria smiled.

Brock took a long drink of some bottled water. He drained the entire bottle before he flopped down — belly first onto the bed. His legs and arms stretched outright.

He was out in seconds.

Quinn and Maria changed out of their beach wear and got into something a little more appropriate for dinner. Maria slipped on another one of her knee high summer dresses. This one was a slinky, little black, satiny one. It had the spaghetti straps like the other one she wore earlier in the day but this one hugged her petite frame even closer. She looked sexy and elegant.

She started working on her hair. She brushed it straight using a flat iron to smooth and flatten it perfectly; so not a strand would be out of place. Then she started working on her makeup. She penciled on some dark black mascara around her eyelids and powdered her face with blush before she smeared some hot, red lipstick on her pouty lips.

Quinn threw on a pair of black cargo shorts, and a white button up, short sleeve, shirt. He stood behind Maria, looking in the mirror. He fiddled with a couple wispy strands of hair so that it would hang just right. He splashed some cologne on his neck — then started rummaging around in his duffle bag for something. Whatever it was he was looking for he found it, and slipped it into his front pocket quickly. He then pulled out a pair of loafers, slipped them on and looked at Maria.

"So are you ready or what?" he asked. He was hungry, but he was also anxious and didn't want to waste anymore time.

Maria stood from in front of the mirror and twisted her little frame from front, to back, and side to side.

She was pretty sure she looked good.

Quinn let out a little growl watching her. It made her smile. That was all she needed to know for certain.

'Yah I look good!' She thought to herself.

Maria slipped on her gladiator heels and smiled at Quinn.

"I'm ready baby!" she replied with a devious smile.

They walked out and locked the door behind them but knocked on Brock's door before going to the elevator. Maria opened it a crack.

"Is he sleeping?" Quinn whispered as Maria poked her head inside.

"Yah he is — let's go." She replied as she looked at Brock sprawled out, face down on the bed. She quietly closed the door.

They took the elevator down to the lobby and left the GPR. They were headed toward 5th Ave. They stopped just outside a quaint little restaurant called Alpastro's. They spent a few moments outside debating whether or not they should eat there. They decided not to in the end because they wanted to take stroll down PDC's main strip (5th Ave) and hopefully find a cozier more authentic Mexican Riviera style restaurant.

A few minutes later they were on 5th Ave.

They were hoping to look inside a few of the stores but few were still open. It was getting close to 6pm and the sun was beginning to fade. They walked for another 10 minutes or so down the main strip on 5th Ave, looking for a restaurant.

They came across a couple restaurants but none of them caught their interest and so they continued down the strip, until one in particular jumped out at them. It wasn't so much the restaurant itself that caught their eye. It was because they ran into Miguel Sanchez their limo driver from this morning.

Miguel happened to be outside the front doors of a place called the Blue Manikou. He must have been waiting for some other clients. It looked busy and the Caribbean music that played in the background was loud enough that they could hear it from across the street.

They waved and shouted hello to Miguel. He waved back at them and shouted "Hola". Just then a group of people came out, and he got distracted. Miguel helped the group into his limo but looked back to see Quinn and Maria enter the Blue Manikou.

Quinn and Maria walked inside and got a table for two almost immediately. They were seated off in one of the corners across from the bar counter where lots of people were sitting and standing around. The music that played in the background offered a warm and cozy Mexican feel to the atmosphere.

Maria ordered a margarita and Quinn ordered a Corona to start off with. The waitress brought them their drinks within minutes and asked if they were ready to order. The menu was limited to five items.

They decided on a plate of sautéed shrimp and a garden salad each. The waitress took their orders and left them to themselves.

"So are you having a good time baby?" Quinn asked her as he reached his hand to the center of the table to hold hers.

"Yes — I feel so relaxed and at peace right now." she responded and slid her little hand inside his. She tilted her head to one side slightly. There was a strange look in his eyes. He was staring at her deeply and looked like he wanted to say something.

"Is everything ok?" Maria asked.

Quinn's stomach was filled with butterflies. He reached his other hand into his front pocket under the table. It was the same pocket he had slipped something into from his duffle bag before they had left room.

"Listen." Quinn said and paused for a second. "I keep thinking that there will be this perfect time and place." He started to talk again but stopped. "But you know — I now realize that there is no such perfect time or place because no matter where or when it is — it always feels like it's the perfect time or place." He continued.

Maria's face looked a little puzzled as he said this to her. She wasn't really sure if she was following what he was saying.

Quinn leaned forward a little closer to her and whispered "What I'm trying to say Maria — is that I love you. I love every minute I spend with you, and I love the thought of spending the rest of my life with you."

Maria's eyes widened. Her heart started to beat like a heavy drum. "Was he actually proposing?" She could feel her blood surge and a heat rush up her neck to her cheeks and forehead. Her breath quickened, and her stomach was now filled with butterflies too.

Quinn pulled out a large diamond engagement ring. It was a solitaire diamond, attached to a white gold band. It was his mothers. He had held on to it for all these years—since he was 5 years old. He inherited it after she died, and it was the only solid thing he ever had to remember his mother by, aside from some photographs. The diamond was enormous. It was a 10 karat Canadian diamond. It sparkled and flashed like a disco ball as the flame of the candle in the center of the table flickered romantically. He gently held her finger outright and straight, and placed the ring at the very tip of her finger

"So if you will have me—I want to marry you Maria. With all my heart I want you to be my wife—will you marry me?" he asked in the sincerest of tones.

Maria felt the saliva thicken in her throat. It forced her to take a slow, deep gulp. A wash of tears started to flood her eyes and her heart raced like the third arm of a ticker watch on fast forward.

It was the moment she dreamed of since she was just a young girl. It was her everlasting dream to hear Quinn ask her that one simple question, and it was so like Quinn to say so much more—to speak straight from his heart and to say such kind words that made her melt from the inside out.

"Yes!" was all she could manage to say. Her voice cracked but the tone was pure and genuine. Her body trembled, and she felt light and weak all over.

Quinn's face lit up with a smile hearing her say that one simple word, and he wasted no time sliding the ring up the length of her finger. It fit perfectly. He had it sized months ago after first learning her ring size — one day after Maria dragged him into a jewellery store. When it was on, they both took a moment to gaze at it on her tiny finger. It looked amazing. A moment later, they leaned over the table and melted their mouths into each others, and sealed their engagement with a long, loving kiss.

∞∞∞∞

Chapter 9

Tonya's thoughts wander

After Sandra and Tonya dropped Luke off at the GPR, they drove back home to Sandra's. It was only a 15 minute drive away. They didn't say much to each other the whole ride back. Sandra was busy talking on her cell phone to one of her colleagues. She was telling him to get in contact with the property owner and have them draw up a sales contract right away. She was so excited. She was so close to finalizing the sale that she was speaking a mile a minute.

Tonya felt ignored and even though it annoyed her, she was used to it. It had been that way ever since her father died when she was only ten years old and her mother remarried Dan Marx just six months later. She figured she should just be happy that she had a few hours to talk heart to heart with her mother last night when she first arrived. By the looks of things she wouldn't have a chance to have too many more conversations like that with her mother now that she was about to land a huge, multi million dollar deal.

Dan Marx (Tonya's stepfather) was a chauvinistic, crude, prick that treated her mother like a piece of shit.

He was both physically and emotionally abusive. He even came on to Tonya when she was just 17. Tonya threatened to go to the police if he ever touched her like he did again. He took off, leaving Tonya's mother with nothing but a broken heart and a low self esteem. Tonya never did tell her mother why he left or what happened.

A year later Tonya left for University.

Tonya hated him, and she hated the fact that her mother extended her last name to Marx when she was just 13 years old. Yet she grew up hearing people tell her that her name sounded like it was a famous person's name. Tonya Wells-Marx — *it did have a nice ring to it* — but it was the principal of the matter, it was the last name of a dirty pig of a man. Oddly enough though, she decided to keep it, only because she thought it might stand out in the world of fashion, and help her career chances.

It seemed to be working for her so far.

Sandra left for Mexico shortly after the break up. It was only supposed to be a two week vacation but after coming to Playa Del Carmen, and not really having anything left to go back to in the US; with Tonya being in college, and after having sold the house — she decided to stay.

It was turning out to be one of the wisest decisions she ever made.

Four years later here she was, living in paradise with a budding career, and a bright future.

Tonya slumped down on the sofa. She was a little tired but she was also restless. That was the first time she had been out in PDC, and the sun felt so good on her skin. She doubted her mother would have much time to do anything over the next day or so while trying to make this sale go through.

Sandra scurried around the loft still talking on her cell. Tonya stood from the sofa and went to the kitchen. She opened the refrigerator door and looked for something to snack on. There wasn't much–a half empty bottle of milk, half a loaf of bread, a head of lettuce, butter, and a few condiments like ketchup and mustard.

Tonya grimaced and opened the crisper and found three apples. She grabbed the reddest one of the three and shut the refrigerator door. She found a shaker of salt, and a sharp paring knife, and walked back to the living room and slumped back down on the sofa.

Tonya dug the knife into the apple and slowly started twisting the apple round and round until it was peeled. The apple peel came off as one curly strand. It looked like a spring as she held it up for a second looking at it with a small amount of pride and accomplishment. She then placed it on the end table beside her. She sprinkled some salt on the apple and then began to slice a piece off. She brought it to her mouth.

Tonya's mind started to wander as she slowly chewed on piece after piece.

Tonya's thoughts wandered to that far off distant place in her mind where fairy tales and fantasies came true. She was thinking of her day out today, thinking of her brief encounter with Luke. Thinking of how she acted around him. Tonya was on her best behavior but she kept it real–as real as she could keep it. Her thoughts started to wander deeper. "*I wonder what tonight might be like?*" She asked herself. Luke had asked her and her mother to join him for dinner while he looked over some price comparisons of other properties similar to the property he was prepared to buy.

Tonya started thinking of wine and candle lights–maybe even sharing a sweet cuddle beneath the stars and moon on the beach. '*Luke didn't seem to be such a bad guy but he was different from most of the guys she knew.*' He just seemed so confident, and a tad bit arrogant.

The other thing was that, she wasn't used to being around someone who was so wealthy–*wealthier than she could ever imagine being.* He did however manage to make her laugh and even blush a couple times while they were checking out the property. Yet no matter how hard she tried, Tonya couldn't stop thinking of the handsome man with long, wavy, black hair and deep, warm, blue eyes she walked past earlier in the GPR lobby.

Her thoughts wandered until the apple was down to the core. She stood up from the sofa again, and grabbed the apple peel and walked back into the kitchen. She threw the core and the peel in the garbage and placed the knife into the sink. She grabbed a bottle of water from the refrigerator — opened it, and took a small sip. It was cold and refreshing. She twisted the lid back on, and again she walked back to the sofa, and set down the bottle of water on the end table.

Tonya's eyes began to slowly close as she listened to her mother yap on her cell like a mad woman cranked up and wired on too much caffeine. She almost felt like taking a nap just so that she didn't have to listen to her anymore but her eyes just so happened to glance at a magazine that was sitting on the coffee table. It was of a bare-chested guy with washboard abs. It caught her attention because the guy on the cover of the magazine had the same long, black, wavy hair as the guy she seen earlier this morning walking into the GPR lobby.

She picked up the magazine to take a closer look. "Oh my God — that's him!" She squealed silently inside her head.

Her jaw dropped an inch or so in disbelief. It wasn't just his hair that seemed to have burned itself into her memory — it was his eyes. It was those deep, calm, blue eyes that were unforgettable to her. She had never seen such deep blue eyes on anyone before.

There he was! Bare-chested posing on the cover of the 'Million Dollar Yachts' magazine. The cover title read, "*Get up close and personal with Brock Castegere — Billionaire and lead designer of C&B's most luxurious yachts!*" and in small print at the bottom of the cover page it referred to "*page 33 for the whole story*".

She quickly flipped to page 33 and started reading.

∞∞∞∞

Chapter 10

The Blue Manikou

April 23rd, 2010. 5:45 pm CST.

Jacob Stanley's cell phone beeped. It was a message from Luke that read, "Something came up, see you tomorrow." A minute later his cell beeped again. It said incoming media. He clicked to receive it and then a picture file appeared. It was from one of his contacts. The picture showed two guys *(Brock and Quinn)* and one very petite beautiful caramel color haired girl *(Maria)* standing in front of the GPR.

Jacob studied her for a few minutes then scrolled down to the bottom of the picture. There was a message that read, "She's at the Blue Manikou now."

Jacob tossed the cell on the coffee table. He cracked open a can of beer after putting a DVD into the player then slumped back into the white, leather sofa inside the yacht. He grabbed a remote and pointed it to the 50" flat screen LCD TV console mounted on the wall in front of him.

The DVD started playing. *It was a home made video.* Jacob guzzled down the can of beer and let out a loud burp followed by an *"Ahhh…"* and set the can down on the glass coffee table in front of him.

One of Jacob's hands reached down inside his shorts. He grabbed his crotch and started to squeeze himself. *"Mmm…"* he moaned *"I still remember you honey."*

Jacob watched a young woman who could have been no more than 20 walk into a room with a king size bed. It was the master room in the yacht. She was holding a bottle of wine and was obviously drunk–*stumbling over drunk*–as she flopped down on the edge of it wearing only a bikini.

The frame cut and then it showed the girl lying face down on the king bed. *She was passed out.* She was noticeably petite and thin. Jacob flashed the hand held camera back and forth between her and himself. The anticipation of what he was leading up to was nauseating.

Jacob was still holding the camera when he climbed on the bed behind the girl. It showed him slowly sliding her bikini bottom down and eventually off. How he carefully raised her hips so that she was on her knees and her butt was lifted in the air. He moved the camera so that it was showing a clear view of her exposed bottom from behind. *It was Jacob's point of view.* He started touching her and rubbing her — it was obvious she wasn't even aware of it at first.

The girl was so drunk she didn't know what was going on. It went on for a few minutes like that, until he shifted the focus of the camera onto his penis. He angled the camera so it showed one of his hands spreading apart her butt cheeks. From there a slow 5 minutes passed of watching him press the head of his penis against her opening. He was slowly trying to work it inside of her. It was agonizing to watch and it was even more disturbing hearing the moans and eventual painful cries she made.

It carried on for at least 10 minutes before the video went black
.

Jacob grabbed a towel and wiped the semen off his belly. He had a smile on his face. That girl in the video was one of his latest victims that he had picked up just a few days ago.

Jacob stood up and walked to the washroom and turned on the shower. When he finished showering, five or ten minutes later, he slipped on a short sleeved Hawaiian shirt, some army green cargo pants, and a pair of runners.

Jacob opened his night table drawer and pulled out a small 9mm Glock19 and tucked it behind his back securing it between the waist band of his pants and his lower back. He grabbed a money roll. It was two thousand dollars worth, all in US twenties. There were a few of them rolling around in the drawer. He tossed the roll into the air, and watched it twirl a couple of times before it dropped back into the palm of his hand. He tucked it into one of his front pockets. There was also a pill bottle with a bunch of ruffies inside. He quickly stuffed the pill bottle into his other pocket.

Jacob shut the night table drawer and walked out of the bedroom–grabbed his cell phone on the coffee table and clipped it onto the hip of his pants. He climbed up to the deck, and then started down the ladder on the port side of the yacht.

He was headed for the Blue Manikou on 5th Ave.

Jacob quickly made his way into town from the docks. It was only a few minutes away. The sun was just starting to set and it was nearly 7pm. He was looking for some action because he was in the mood again.

About five minutes later Jacob arrived at the Blue Manikou. Caribbean music was playing in the background and people were filing into it by the dozens. He walked inside, and headed straight for the bar. He ordered a Corona and guzzled half of the bottle down before taking a good, long look around.

There were lots of young college aged girls and guys inside–mainly American tourists. Some were up in the center floor dancing to the rhythm of the upbeat Caribbean jive playing over the speakers. Others were seated at cozy tables having candle lit dinners. Others were downing shots of tequila getting more and more intoxicated.

Across the floor sitting in one of the corners of the lounge, he spotted a young couple sitting quietly at a table for two (*It was Quinn and Maria*) — and they were clutching each others hands in the center of the table. He guessed they were somewhere in their early to mid twenties. *They looked happy together.* The large diamond engagement ring on the young woman's hand said it all. The empty plates on their table told Jacob they had been here a little while.

Jacob reached for his cell on his hip and brought up the picture he received from his contact. It was definitely her. There was no mistaking that caramel brown color of her hair and her petite little frame. Her hair was perfectly styled and looked enticing as it hung down past her shoulders, and halfway down her back. It was a sexy, young and posh hair style.

Jacob closed his cell and clipped it back to the waist of his pants. He watched her patiently as the flickers of the candle light made her face glow and shimmer, and her deep blue eyes dazzle like sapphires. He studied her closely, enthralled with that sweet, lithe look that a woman gets when she's just been proposed to. Her face was glowing. She was hopelessly in love and it was a look that Jacob couldn't resist.

Jacob barely even looked at Quinn. He wasn't concerned about him. He just glanced at him and made up his own mind that he was a flop. Quinn had that shoulder length messy beach blond hair, a surfer dude look.

Jacob couldn't have cared less what he *(Quinn)* looked like or what she *(Maria)* might have seen in him to be engaged to him. All Jacob was concerned with was how she looked, and how badly he wanted her. He finished his Corona after guzzling the rest of it down, and ordered another one right away for himself. He also ordered them a drink. He could tell what they were drinking.

She was drinking a margarita and her partner was drinking a Corona.

Jacob had the bar tender open the corona and pour the margarita in front of him, and leave them there on the bar in front of him. He reached into his pocket and twisted the cap of the pill bottle that he had stuffed in his pocket from his night table. From inside his pocket he emptied two pills into the palm of his hand, and then twisted the cap back on the pill bottle. He crushed one of the ruffies in the palm of his bare hand just by squeezing with a little force, and then proceeded to sprinkle it into the margarita. He did the same with the other pill and sprinkled that one into the bottle of corona. Jacob made sure no one was watching him.

No one was.

Nobody was paying attention to him. He was experienced at doing this. He'd done it in places a hundred times more crowded than this place was. He waited for another minute to let the crushed ruffies dissolve before he picked up the two drinks and gently began to swirl them in slow, patient, circles.

A couple of minutes passed before Jacob called the bar tender back over and asked him if he could have a waitress send the drinks on over to the young couple in the corner.

Jacob explained that they were engaged, and so he just wanted to congratulate them. He slipped the bar tender a few twenties that he pulled from his money roll.

No one ever did anything out of kindness in downtown PDC—hand them some American bills though—they would bend over backwards for you.

The bar tender whistled for a waitress to come over. In Hispanic he told her to bring the drinks over to the couple in the corner, and to congratulate them on their engagement. Jacob slipped away from the bar counter and swiftly blended himself into the crowds of people that were now starting to file into the place by the droves. He was out of sight and out of mind within seconds. By the time the bar tender looked back over to where Jacob was—he was gone. The bartender just shrugged and went about serving the next patron.

Jacob watched Quinn and Maria thank the waitress politely with big appreciative smiles. "Like feeding nuts to squirrels" He mused to himself.

Jacob chuckled as he watched them clink their drinks together after making a toast. Jacob slowly wiggled his way through the crowded floor toward them–taking his time, he held onto his Corona tightly in one hand, keeping it raised as he tried not to bump into anyone. He didn't want any chance for a scene to happen.

An evil grin grew wide across his face as he watched them take sip after sip, and his heart started beating faster and harder in his demented sense of excitement.

The night had taken over from the daylight hours now. It was almost 7:30 pm. The sun had set, and the party was moving outside to the beach. It was beach club time at the Blue Manikou. A DJ got on the microphone outside and cranked up the volume and introduced himself.

The DJ started off the night with an American hip hop flavor; the song Caribou Lou from Tech N9ne started playing,

"Yeah it's like the ultimate party favor baby ya know.
Two cups will get a hot one out of her clothes ya know.
Caribou Lou
It's like
151 rum
Pineapple juice, and Malibu, caribou, get them all numb
Make baby girl come
Out of her shell and raise hell
Don't stop till the cops come"

-Tech N9ne

ooooo

Chapter 11

Dinner with Luke

April 23rd, 2010. 6:00 pm CST.

Luke was already seated at a table he reserved for a party of 3 at the Alpastro's restaurant. He just finished messaging Jacob telling him that he would see him tomorrow. He decided to spend the night at the resort. He just needed some alone time—not only that—there was always the possibility he might be able to entice Tonya on a date with him this evening.

Luke spent the better part of the afternoon on the beach tanning while drinking dry gin on ice. He went for a few quick dives in the ocean to cool down every now and then. When he had enough of that, he spent some time in the spa, and finally had a long relaxing massage. After that he purchased a pair of socks and running shoes in the clothing boutique inside the resort and retired to his room where he showered and took a short half hour nap.

When Luke woke up it was 5:30 pm. He splashed some water on his face until he felt awake and fixed his hair a little so it didn't look like he just woke up. He pulled on his new socks and threw on his new shoes. He threw on some clothes and checked himself out in the in the tall mirror that was hanging on the wall just beside the door.

Luke left his room feeling satisfied with how he looked and went downstairs taking the stairwell rather than the elevator. The stairwell led to the sidewalk just outside the lobby of the resort. A two minute walk away was the Alpastro's restaurant which was attached to the GPR. He entered the Alpastro's and the hostess quickly had him seated after he tipped her with a hundred dollar bill.

6:00 pm exactly rolled around–when Sandra and her daughter Tonya were escorted to Luke's table. Luke stood from his chair as they approached the table and pulled out a chair for Tonya while the host pulled the other one out for Sandra. The host introduced them to their waiter Roberto, and bid them farewell.

They all smiled and exchanged nods to one another.

"I'm glad you made it." He said as he looked at Tonya first, then at her mother Sandra.

"Thank you!" they both responded at the same time.

Roberto their waiter placed the menus in front of each of them and poured them each a glass of ice water. He then stood back and asked in his Mexican accent "May I get you anything before you order?"

Luke looked at Tonya and Sandra and tilted his hand,

"Red, white wine, champagne?" he asked.

"Champagne would be fitting." Sandra replied.

Tonya just smiled and nodded.

"Champagne it is." Luke looked up at Roberto and said, "Bring us a bottle of your best champagne."

"Of course sir!" Roberto said and quickly left to retrieve a bottle for them.

"So how was the rest of your day Mr. Cassalon?" Sandra asked

"It was nice. I relaxed the whole day. I haven't done that in awhile."

"That's great!" Sandra smiled.

Luke looked at them both and said, "And how was the rest of yours?"

"It was ok." They both answered as one again. They laughed at their timing. Luke just smirked.

"I hope you brought those papers?" Luke asked.

"I did. I wouldn't have forgotten those!" Sandra said with a small laugh. "Did you want to look at them now or wait?" she asked.

"I can take a look at them now." Luke said.

Sandra leaned over and pulled up her purse and placed it on her lap.

Luke turned to Tonya and smiled.

"I like your dress." He whispered.

Tonya was wearing a short, cobalt blue dress that softly draped over her body like how a night slip would look. She was wearing a different set of heels but still 5 inch ones. They were black and had twisting straps that criss-crossed her ankles tightly.

Tonya gave him a sweet smile. "Thank you. I like your shoes."

Luke laughed. "Oh you noticed them did you?" he turned in his seat and lifted his leg off the ground and twisted his foot from side to side showing the shoe off to Tonya.

Sandra at this point felt like a third wheel. She almost wished she could just leave the two of them alone for dinner but she had to finalize the deal.

"Here they are." Sandra said as she pulled the papers out from her purse.

Luke turned back around in his seat and took the papers from Sandra and started to look them over.

—

There were a couple of minutes of silence as he studied the papers. Sandra nudged Tonya under the table with her toe and kept raising her brows excitedly.

Tonya gave her mother a look as to say, "Stop it!!!"

Sandra couldn't help herself though. She was too excited, and wound up inside. This would be her biggest sale yet.

"Looks good, where do I sign, Sandra?" Luke asked and looked up at her.

Sandra's jaw dropped. *That's it? Just like that? He's going to hand three million dollars over just like that?* She was in shock.

"I... I have the papers for you to sign right here Mr. Cassalon" she stuttered. "As soon as you sign those I can call him." She quickly gathered her composure, even though her body was trembling. Her heart was racing. She could feel herself heating up to the point where she thought she was going to break out in a sweat. She handed him a different set of papers, her hand was shaking a little.

Luke noticed her hand shaking but didn't say anything.

He took the papers from her.

"Do you have a pen?" he asked as he read the papers he was about to sign. It was just a lot of legal mumbo jumbo about how if the property owner agreed to the amount that Luke offered; Luke would be legally bound to pay.

Luke continued to read making sure there were no loopholes or fine print he didn't agree with.

He didn't find anything.

Sandra handed him a pen and took out her cell phone and placed it on the table in front of her.

Just then Roberto their waiter returned with a bottle of Dom Perignon.

"I hope this will do?" Roberto asked as he presented it to them holding it delicately in his hands; one hand at the base of it, the other on the neck of it, and tilted it back with the label facing them.

Sandra and Tonya looked at it and smiled, they weren't really sure what, if anything they should say. They just smiled and nodded and hoped Luke would give the ok.

Luke barely glanced up at Roberto and the bottle that he was holding.

"That's fine." He mumbled as he was still preoccupied reading through the papers he was about to sign.

Roberto twisted a corkscrew into the bottle and uncorked it; he proceeded to pour each of them a half glass of wine.

"I'll return in a few moments to take your orders." He said and left their table.

Tonya occupied herself by reading the menu. It was an international menu. She wasn't really all that hungry and was planning on just having a salad. There was a Chicken Caesar salad listed on the menu and she decided she would go with that.

Sandra was shaking but desperately trying to calm herself. She picked up the glass of champagne and took a tiny sip from it. It might have been a little impolite, she wasn't sure if it was or wasn't but she was beyond caring about courtesy. He was going to sign the papers and she was going to close the sale.

About ten minutes passed before Luke finished reading the papers over. He didn't find anything to cause him alarm. It was all pretty straight forward. He needed to put the amount he was offering on one line. Sign his name on another line, and date it.

Luke pressed the pen to the paper and scribbled the amount of 2.5 million dollars. He signed his name and dated it. It was done and he handed the papers back to Sandra.

"Do your magic Sandra. I hope he takes it." He said.

Sandra reached for her cell and flipped it open. She thumbed through her contacts until she found the number she was looking for.

Roberto returned to their table just as Sandra was about to make the call.

"May I take your orders now?" he asked.

Luke looked at Tonya who was just folding her menu closed. "Do you know what you're getting?" he asked.

Luke had it in his mind that he was going to order whatever she did. He wasn't even that hungry either. He just wanted to get the sale over and done with, and hopefully spend the rest of the night with Tonya.

"Yes." Tonya answered with a smile. She looked up at Roberto. "I'll just have the Chicken Caesar salad."

Roberto scribbled her order down on his pad. He paused looking at her. "Anything else Miss?" he asked.

"No that's fine — thanks." Tonya politely replied.

"I'll have the same, except bring us some uh... garlic bread for the table please and thank you" Luke cut in.

Roberto looked to Luke and scribbled his request down. "Very good." then he looked to Sandra.

Sandra had not pressed the call button on her phone yet. She looked up at Roberto and said, "I'll just have whatever they're having." Then she pressed the talk button.

Roberto scribbled their orders down, and repeated them, "So... that's an order of garlic bread and 3 Chicken Caesar Salads?"

"That's right." Luke confirmed.

Roberto smiled at all of them, than left their table to give their orders to the kitchen.

The phone rang three times before a male voice answered on the other end, "Hola!"

Sandra felt a knot of excitement forming in her stomach, and her heart raced a little faster.

"Hola! Un momento por favor" Sandra replied in Mexican. She pulled the phone away from her ear, and looked to Luke. "Do you mind? I'll just be a few minutes." She asked and stood from her chair.

"Not at all — go ahead. Take your time." Luke said. He was feeling really laid back and nonchalant right now.

"Thanks." Sandra whispered before excusing herself from the table. She walked outside of the restaurant and stood on the sidewalk. She was soon engaged in a Spanish conversation with the voice on the other end of the call. She was trying to negotiate from the 3 million dollar asking price down to the 2.5 million Luke was offering.

"So do you have any plans for later?" Luke asked Tonya.

She was waiting for him to ask her that. She flashed him a sweet smile.

"No. I don't have any plans tonight." She replied leaving him ample room to ask her outright on a date.

There was a brief pause of silence. She wondered if he was going to just leave it at that. *"Maybe he wasn't all that into me?"* she wondered as a quick moment of self doubt flashed into her mind.

"I wish I did though." She said suggestively not allowing any room to question later whether he was into her or not. If he didn't ask her out after just saying that to him, then there would be no question that he wasn't that into her.

Tonya barely knew Luke but it was her mother's idea to introduce them to each other in the first place and now that she met him, she kind of liked him. He really did seem charming. They shared a few laughs already, and they were able to hold conversation well. Yet also, somewhere in the back of her mind there was the slightest of thought, of the possibility that she would run into Brock Castegere, the multi billionaire she read about this afternoon, and saw walking past her in the lobby of GPR earlier this morning.

Luke smiled. Tonya really did make the opening easy for him to ask her out on a date.

"Well I have the rest of the night, myself. Maybe we can share a few drinks, maybe catch one of those dance shows at the resort, or even go dancing?" he asked casually.

"I'd like that." She replied with a big smile. She didn't hesitate for a second. She took another drink of her champagne.

"Lovely." Luke said with a pleased smile.

Roberto returned to the table with three platters of Chicken Caesar Salad, and a plate of sliced garlic bread.

"Enjoy your meals." He said after placing their plates in front of each of them. He smiled and walked away.

"Should we start without her?" Tonya asked.

Luke shrugged his shoulders and said, "It's a salad–I don't think she'd mind, do you?" he asked and paused for second.

"But then again—she is your mother—you should know?" He questioned with a chuckle.

"No she won't mind." Tonya laughed. She was pretty certain her mother wouldn't mind.

"Are you sure?" Luke asked as he dug his fork into a chunk of chicken and some lettuce. He saw a slight expression of doubt flash across Tonya's face. He brought his fork close to his mouth and opened his mouth wide. He was just waiting for her to respond before taking that first bite.

Tonya giggled watching him. *"He really was a funny and down to earth guy."* she thought.

"I'm sure!" she said after letting him hang for a few seconds longer.

As soon as she said that, Luke stuffed the fork with chicken and lettuce in his mouth. He looked at her with a big grin on his face as he chewed it slowly.

A half hour later, they both were finished their salads, almost all the garlic bread, and finished the bottle of Dom. Sandra still had not returned to the table.

Luke ordered another bottle and they engaged themselves in conversations about the Mayan Riviera mostly. They talked about how beautiful it was and how Luke had been living in the Caribbean for the past few years, and how much he loved it.

Tonya on the other hand was telling him all about her years spent studying fashion in University, in New York.

Sandra finally returned to the table and her face was beaming. "Well "Mr. Cassalon, I just spoke with the property owner, and..." she paused and took her seat back at the table.

Sandra glanced at her plate of soggy salad

.

"And...?" Luke asked. He was anticipating good news.

"Congratulations! He accepted the offer!" She blurted out, unable to hold back the suspense any longer.

"That's wonderful Sandra" Luke responded with a broad smile. He extended his hand to shake on it with her.

Tonya smiled and pressed her hands together and let her fingertips touch her chin. "Yay!" she exclaimed.

"That's great news you guys!" she said and winked at her mom. She was proud that her mom made the sale. She knew how badly her mom wanted it.

"Thank you." Sandra said and paused for a second. "We just need to meet up tomorrow afternoon with him and his agent to seal the deal—so to speak." She paused again and looked at Luke with a serious look in her eyes. "That's not going to be a problem for you is it? I mean the transaction will need to take place at that time–in cash as we agreed."

Luke chuckled. "That's not going to be a problem Sandra." he assured her.

Just then Roberto returned to the table with the second bottle of Dom, and a new clean glass for Sandra. He had noticed earlier that her glass had been sitting there untouched the whole time.

He poured them each a new glass and set the bottle on the center of the table. He then proceeded to clean the table taking Luke and Tonya's empty plates away but before he reached for Sandra's plate he asked her, "Should I take this away Ma'am?"

"Oh yes, please." She replied wrinkling her nose as she looked at the shriveled up lettuce.

"Did you want a new plate?" Roberto asked knowing it had not been touched.

"No, that's fine. Thank you though."

"Are you sure you're not hungry Sandra?" Luke asked.

"Positive. My stomach is too full of butterflies right now anyways." She explained. "I'll just have a piece or two of this garlic bread, but thank you all the same."

Roberto took her untouched plate of food and hurried away with their dishes.

Luke raised his glass again ready to propose another toast, "To you Sandra, for all your excellent work."

Tonya and Sandra raised their glasses and they all clashed their glasses together and took a sip. "Great work mom. I'm proud of you." Tonya added.

They had a few more glasses of the Dom until the bottle was finished again. Their conversation was light hearted and easy for the remainder of their time at the table. They mostly talked about what a great investment this was going to be for Luke.

Luke waived Roberto over and asked for the bill. He was going to pay for it, and he wasn't going to waste anytime in bickering over that. He didn't care what the bill came to; he just wanted to end the dinner so that he and Tonya could get on with their night out together.

Roberto swiftly hurried back with the bill and lingered beside Luke for a moment. Luke pulled a clip of money from his front pocket. It was a thick fold of hundreds. He was carrying several thousands on him.

Luke just glanced at the total, out of mere curiosity. It came to $322.00. Tonya caught sight of the wad of money Luke was holding and blinked looking at her mom with a stunned look on her face that she tried to hide with a sheepish smile.

"Roberto you were fantastic!" Luke said.

"Thank you very much sir." Roberto responded. His eyes were fixated on the fold of money in Luke's hands as well. He appreciated the compliment but would appreciate a few of the bills Luke had in hands even more.

Luke slid out five one hundred dollar bills, paused for a moment and then slid one more out of his fold, and handed them to Roberto.

"Great job tonight Roberto. I mean that." Luke said with an honest smile and handed him the 6 one hundred dollar bills.

Roberto's eyes widened with both appreciation and surprise. That was the biggest tip he ever received from one table so far. He took the money and bid them good night as they all stood from the table.

They walked out of the Alpastro's restaurant and loitered on the sidewalk outside for a minute.

"Well I guess we'll see you tomorrow Sandra." Luke said looking up and down the street for Sandra's parked SUV.

"Yes, remember we have to meet him at his office at 3:00pm tomorrow." Sandra reminded him of the time.

"Of course and I'll meet you in the lobby again at 2:00pm sharp. That should leave us plenty of time to get there right?"

"Oh definitely, his office isn't too far. Fifteen or twenty minutes, tops."

"Perfect. So where are you parked?" Luke asked, still looking around for her SUV.

"Oh we parked over in the lot across the way there." Tonya jumped in pointing toward the parking lot across the street.

They started walking toward it after crossing the street. Luke looked at Tonya, he wondered if she was going to tell her mother that she was going to stay behind with him, or if he should.

Tonya looked at Luke and was wondering the same thing. They shared a knowing laugh together — almost like they were reading each others thoughts. She was already feeling a little tipsy after having at least 5 glasses of Dom-the giggles were erupting from her lips easily.

Sandra looked at the two of them trailing behind her a step or two as they shared their laugh together. "Did I miss something?" she asked.

They reached the SUV and stopped.

"No nothing." Luke shook his head trying to wipe the smile from his face.

"Well mom, I'm just going to stay out awhile, Luke and I, were just saying how nice it would be to share a couple drinks and watch the dance show playing tonight at the GPR." Tonya finally confided.

Sandra's eyes widened a little and looked from Tonya to Luke and then back to Tonya. She smiled and nodded her head. "Alright then…" she said, pausing briefly. "Well you two have fun." She suddenly felt more like a mother than a broker after a big sale. "I trust you'll have her back at a decent time?"

Luke felt the same shift in her personality change. Sandra was wearing the parent hat now. He didn't really care — Tonya was an adult, and in his opinion he just paid Sandra a big chunk of money in commission, it was more than she probably would make in two or three years. He felt entitled.

"I'll try my best." was all that Luke could offer to her.

"Don't worry mom, I'm a big girl." Tonya laughed. She felt a little uncomfortable suddenly. Here she was going on a date with a complete stranger practically. Not to mention she had told her mother just last night that she didn't want to go on a date with anyone.

Sandra looked back at Tonya and smiled. "Yes I know dear." She paused for a moment and leaned over to give her daughter a small hug, and then looked at them both. She felt a strange worry come over her suddenly. He could have said *"I will."* She thought to herself. 'Would that have been so hard?' That would have been the gentlemanly thing to say to a parent. Tonya was right though. She wasn't a child anymore. She was 22 years old. She was a young level headed woman who had grown up quite a lot this past year.

"Okay then. You two have a good time, and be, good!" Sandra added. She opened the door to her SUV and slid herself inside it. She closed the door and rolled her window half way down and waved at them

"Call me if you need to." Sandra shouted to Tonya as she drove off.

"Okay, I will." Tonya shouted back and waved to her as she drove off.

∞∞∞∞

Chapter 12

Brock awakens

April 23rd, 2010. 8:12pm CST.

Brock's eyes flashed open and focused on the red LED lights of the alarm clock that was sitting on the night table. It was 8:12pm. His head was hung half off the side of the bed and a long stain of drool was visibly soaked into the sheets. He laid there dazed and disoriented not moving so much as a muscle. It took a few moments to register where he was, and as soon as it did, he sprung up from the bed and sat up on the side of it. He gave his head a shake trying to clear it of all the sleepy cob webs.

"Ah shit!" he groaned still feeling groggy and half a sleep.

Brock took a big breath and stood from the bed, stretched his arms out, and yawned. He walked over to the front window of his room that was right beside the door and stuck his fingers through the vertical blinds and pulled them down making a hole to look through. It was dark outside and the white shaded patio lights strung on the veranda railing outside his room were lit. He looked back at the digital alarm clock on the night table and realized he had slept for about three hours.

Brock's mouth was dry and he felt a little dehydrated. He turned around and walked over to the little bar fridge under the desk on the wall opposite of his queen sized bed. He grabbed a bottle of water and guzzled it down in one drink. He tossed it in the garbage pale and walked into the washroom, and turned the shower on. He stripped off his clothes and got in.

Five minutes later Brock stepped out of the shower and dried himself off with a towel before wrapping it around his hips. He grabbed a toothbrush and started to brush his teeth. As he looked at himself in the mirror he could see already how much sun he got from earlier today. When he was finished brushing his teeth, he walked back into the bedroom and reached for his duffle bag and pulled out some clean clothes.

Brock dressed himself quickly and went back into the washroom. He pressed his fingers into a container the hair balm he brought with him and fingered it through his loose locks of black hair. He then reached for a bottle of Aqua Di Gio cologne and rubbed some in his palms and then all over his neck. He studied himself in the mirror for a minute. He looked good, felt good, and was ready to take on the night now. He slipped on his shoes and left his room.

Brock knocked on Maria and Quinn's door after locking his.

"Hey are you guys in there?" He called out leaning his face closer to their door. He paused and waited for a response. Nothing–he knocked again.

"Hey! Are you guys there?" He called out again. *"Alright then..."* he mumbled to himself as there still wasn't a response. He walked away toward the elevator.

It was 8:30pm when Brock stepped off the elevator.

The inside buffet restaurant had just closed for the evening. Brock was hungry and needed to eat something.

———

"*Just wonderful*" Brock muttered to himself. He decided to try his luck at the bar and lounge, and was relieved to find that they were still serving something at least.

Brock ordered the plate of nachos & cheese with salsa, along with a corona. In minutes he was stuffing his mouth with nachos and kept glancing around hoping he'd see Quinn and Maria. He had no such luck. He was starting to feel a little ticked off that they let him sleep so long but he kept telling himself that they'd show up soon, and when they did, they would have some fun together.

Brock noticed that there were quite a few people heading out back to the pool area and the outside bar. There was stage set up, and he noticed people dressed in dance costumes running in and out of the doors preparing for the evening entertainment. "Maybe they were already out there sitting at a table?" He wondered.

He'd check it out when he was done eating. Even if Quinn and Maria weren't out there at least he'd have something to occupy his time until they found each other again. Surely -they'd look out there for him when they got back from where ever they were.

∞∞∞∞

Chapter 13

Taken

Jacob took his time. Just enough time to know that the effects of the ruffies he spiked Quinn and Maria's drinks with was about to start taking effect. They were almost finished their drinks now. He stood just off to the side of their table leaning against a support beam with his back to them. Every so often he would glance over his shoulder at them. He was waiting for their conversation to go quiet. He couldn't make out what they were saying, but he could hear them. He was waiting to see that far off distant look glaze over their eyes. He knew that look. He had seen it many times before.

Jacob gave it another five minutes before he slid himself into the seat beside Maria. He sat there for a minute and didn't say a word. He was looking straight at Quinn. It was like they didn't even notice him there.
Maria just turned her head and looked at him. She was expressionless as he sat down and Quinn just stared at him, blinking slowly.

It was a creepy silence that lasted for a long two minutes.

"The name is Jack." Jacob extended his hand to Quinn over the table after a couple more minutes had passed, he wasn't about to give out his real name no matter how drugged they might have been.

Quinn lifted his arm slowly and shook Jacob's hand. His hand was limp and weightless.

"Quinn" he replied–his voice was listless.

Jacob released his grip on Quinn's hand. Quinn's hand fell to the table like dead weight. Jacob turned his head and looked at Maria and reached for her hand. He had a wide smile as he held her little hand in his.

"Maria." She whispered. Her voice was just as listless as Quinn's was and her eyes were extremely distant.

Jacob didn't let go of her hand and she didn't pull it away but she wasn't even aware that Jacob was holding her hand.

"It's good to meet you." Jacob said still smiling as he guided her hand to his crotch under the table. He squeezed her hand so it wrapped around him over top of his pants. He turned his head to look back at Quinn.

The smile on Jacob's face was wide. He looked wicked and evil as the candle flickered and cast dark streaking shadows up on his face. He was quiet for another few minutes just enjoying the grip Maria had around him on his crotch under the table.

"You're a lucky man Quinn." He blurted out as he looked straight into Quinn's eyes.

A small smirk was all Quinn could manage as a response. He was out of his senses and drifting away quickly.

"But right now you two are looking really bummed you know that?" Jacob continued then paused for another minute. They didn't respond. He wasn't expecting them to either. Jacob could see by the way their heads were starting to bob and wobble that they were about to pass out at any minute.

"Come on I'll show you two a good time. We'll go to my place. I've got a boat not far from here, and we'll party it up." Jacob talked to them as if they were good friends and eerily as if they were actually coherent. He stood up from the table quickly holding onto Maria's hand. He tugged her arm so that she would try to stand up out of her seat.

Quinn's eyes looked up at the two of them standing up from the table. He was barely able to keep his eyes open at this point.

Jacob pulled Maria in close to him and wrapped his arm around her shoulders, and held her close. He was supporting her weight as she was unsteady on her feet. He looked down at Quinn with a smug look on his face.

"Are you sure you don't want to come with us buddy?" he asked in a taunting tone.

Quinn's eyes closed, and his head slumped forward until his chin was touching his chest.

Quinn was out cold.

Jacob laughed. He thought it was hilarious that Quinn was passed out and that he now had his girl.

"…Such a shame. You're going to miss out on all the fun." Jacob taunted with a haughty tone. He leaned down and gave Maria a peck on the top of her head. His mouth moved down to the side of her head and he whispered in a terrifying serious tone into her ear, "I'm going to have so much fun with you, girl… And I promise I'm going to take my time with you."

Jacob then turned and led Maria away from the table. Her head was pressed against his ribs. Her mouth was drooling saliva, and her legs were like noodles as he took her outside into the back where the beach club party was taking place. People were drinking and dancing everywhere.

Jacob kept leading her toward the beach. He turned toward the docks, and eventually the music started to fade into the distance as he kept walking as he lead her away from the Blue Manikou and into the darkness to where there was nothing but the sound of the ocean, splashing waves onto the shore. Jacob scooped Maria up and slung her over his shoulder. He was rushing quickly toward docks now.

∞∞∞∞

Chapter 14

Confrontations

April 23rd, 2010. 9:00 pm CST.

Brock stood up from the lounge bar and headed outside into the back, to watch the nightly entertainment. He looked around for Quinn and Maria but they weren't there. There were 10 tables set out in the front of the dance stage. Some of them were still empty but Quinn and Maria weren't sitting at any of the tables.

"What the fucking hell?" Brock cursed under his breath. He was getting really irritated now. *He almost felt worried.* It just seemed so strange to him that they would leave him alone for so long. He didn't know if he should worry or be angry and was struggling between feeling both.

Brock decided to take a seat at one of the empty tables. He sat behind a couple *(Luke and Tonya).* The girl had long blond hair and the guy had spiky brown hair. She was wearing a really sexy looking cobalt blue dress — or at least it looked sexy from what he could see of it. The guy sitting beside her was in just a plain, white, polo shirt and cargo shorts. He couldn't see their faces just yet. She was sipping on a daiquiri and the guy was drinking either vodka, rum, or gin.

The stage suddenly filled with female dancers dressed in revealing outfits with just enough material on them to cover their private parts. The music started with heavy bass drums and eventually broke into a full Caribbean jive.

Brock took a long swig from his bottle of Corona and finished it. He was trying to concentrate on the show but the blonde lady sitting in front of him kept distracting him. He was attracted to her and kept wishing she would just glance his way. He was only catching sight of her profile from the side. He found it hard to keep his eyes off of her even though he hadn't seen her face yet. The dance ended and that's when heard her soft voice laugh. *He was intrigued.* Her voice sounded so alluring. It was spicy and yet sweet—melodic to his ears. Brock tried to catch her attention by forcing a small cough. She didn't look back. Finally he resorted to a more drastic measure and dropped his bottle off the table.

Tonya looked back. Luke also looked back. Brocks face was flushed, and his jaw dropped seeing her face staring at him. *It was her!* It was the beautiful young lady he seen earlier this morning walking past him in the lobby when he first arrived. It was the girl who smiled like an angel at him before she got into a black SUV.

A waitress came rushing over to Brocks table, as well as a busboy who quickly swept up the broken bottle. The waitress asked if Brock wanted another drink.

Brock was barely listening to her and just nodded his head. He smiled at Tonya, and she was smiling right back at him. Their eyes were locked on each other.

"Hi." Brock gasped.

"Hi." She replied softly.

Both their voices were slow and awkward. The air was thick with their obvious attraction for each other. It was so thick that Luke had to interrupt them.

"Tonya?—Do you two know each other?"

Tonya's eyes blinked as though she was just pulled back into reality from wherever she just was.

"Luke sorry—yes—I mean no..." she was fumbling for words.

Brock blinked back to reality too and jumped into the conversation to save her from fumbling her words.

72

"I'm Brock" he said extending his hand toward Luke.

Luke reluctantly shook his hand, his face looked a little angry and was judging Brock immediately, sizing him up. He felt insulted but was trying to stay cool for the time being.

"So do you two know each other or not?" Luke asked bluntly.

"We've seen each other before — I mean, I saw his picture on the cover of a magazine-oh never mind." Tonya tried explaining before breaking out into laughter.

"Hi — I'm Tonya." She introduced herself to Brock, and held her hand out to him.

"Hello." Brock replied and laughed with her. He was actually surprised that she said that she had seen his picture on a magazine. That could have been either a good thing or a bad thing. It meant she knew he was a billionaire. Yet it also meant that she was looking at his body. He was just happy to be holding her hand at the moment — he didn't care if she knew if he was a billionaire or not — he was captivated with her, and he was just thankful for the opportunity of actually meeting her.

Luke glared at Brock. He wasn't impressed. The attraction Tonya and Brock shared for each other was more than apparent. Luke felt sparks of jealousy flare up inside of him.

The next dance routine started on the stage, and Luke took that opportunity to break up their wanton stares. "Well — no offence to you, but I think we'd like to finish watching the show now." He uttered bluntly yet as politely as he could stomach.

Brock and Tonya were instantly tuned into Luke's discontent and felt him emanating an awkward sense of jealousy in the air. Neither of them wanted to stop talking to each other but it was obvious that Luke wasn't pleased.

"Hey, I'm sorry to have interrupted." Brock said clearing his throat. He thought he'd take the high road and be a gentleman and respect Luke's position.

Luke just nodded and turned in his seat to watch the next dance routine.

Tonya raised her brows and lifted her shoulders and didn't know what to say. She suddenly felt like she was obligated to turn her attention to the stage. She didn't want to, but she was Luke's date after all.

Brock lifted his brows and let out a big sigh, and leaned back in his chair. He was still looking at Tonya, just watching the back of her head, and let his eyes roam down her neck line to her shoulders and down her back. He could tell that she was glancing back at him from out of the corner of her eye.

Tonya was being careful or considerate at least not to let Luke see her eyes trying to glance back to him.

Brock found it a little amusing, but he could understand Luke not wanting another guy moving in on the woman he was with — especially on a woman as beautiful as Tonya. It did make him wonder though if they were a couple or not, and why such a beautiful young woman would allow herself to be tied down by a guy who was so obviously jealous.

The waitress returned to Brocks table with a Corona. Brock reached into his pocked and pulled a one hundred dollar bill out of his money fold.
"Keep them coming — theirs too." He said handing her the bill, and pointed to Tonya and Luke.

The waitress nodded, and took his money before moving over to the table Luke and Tonya were sitting at. When she learned what their drinks were she retreated back to the outside bar to get their drinks.

The second dance routine ended and it went quiet again. Luke had a tick pulsing on the side of his cheek. He wanted to leave but he wasn't going to leave Tonya alone, only to be swooned and likely picked up by Brock. He was thinking of what he could do.

Luke played out many scenarios in his mind. He didn't know Brock. He knew nothing about the guy, other than the fact that Tonya sort of mentioned that he was on a magazine. He certainly didn't know Brock was a billionaire.

"So Brock—is it?" he asked.

Brock took a swig of his Corona and set it down on the table. Tonya turned immediately to face Brock also.

"That's right" Brock replied.

"You were in a magazine?" Luke asked curiously.

Brock chuckled. *Which one?* He thought to himself. He was on the cover of many magazines.

"Yeah that's right. I've been in a few."

"Why?" Luke asked bluntly.

Brock looked at Tonya with a confident look on his face. *"I'm sure she knows."* He thought to himself.

"Just the nature of my business I guess." He replied shrugging his shoulders.

Tonya felt like jumping in at that moment to explain to Luke everything she just read about Brock she wanted to say that *"He was the heir to his father's fortune, and CEO of C&B Inc. He designed the world's most luxurious yachts. He was rated one of the most eligible bachelors in the world. He was young, filthy rich, and rakishly handsome!"* But she hesitated.

Luke didn't like the vague response Brock offered him. "So like a male model or something?" Luke probed further.

Brock laughed. "Something like that... yeah."

Tonya giggled and finally had to interrupt, "He designs yachts, Luke"

Luke shot her a cold look. He was building up to something where he thought he would be able to take a verbal stab at Brock to make him feel small.

"Yachts?" he hissed, thrown completely off guard. It was such an unexpected thing to hear. Luke owned a yacht–*A very expensive one.*

Brock smiled at Tonya and gave her a nod as to say, *Very good!*

"That's right Tonya." He said and paused for a second. He looked back at Luke "I design luxury yachts, and model on occasion." He explained with somewhat of a cocky tone. He knew Tonya most likely seen one of the magazine spreads where he was shirtless and modeling his well sculpted body on the deck of one of his company's multi million dollar yachts.

Luke started putting the pieces of the puzzle together in his head. He knew a lot about yachts. He knew the one he owned was a limited edition C&B special. He knew that only 3 existed in the world. It was designed by the famed Yacht Designer Henry Castegere. It was said to be the pride of all yachts. It was the last yacht designed by Henry before he died 4 years ago.

Luke remembered reading something about how his son, Brock had not only inherited his fortune and share of the company, but also the family genes of yacht design. *"So this is Brock Castegere — multi billionaire, and poster boy of the famous C&B Inc."* Luke thought ruefully to himself. Luke didn't know how to feel at that moment. He was hoping he could have belittled Brock but that clearly was out of the question now. Luke was actually a big yacht enthusiast, and so it changed things a little.

"Brock Castegere?" Luke asked. "The Brock Castegere of C&B Inc.?" He asked more specifically.

Brock's eyes widened. He was surprised. *What were the chances of someone knowing?* One person recognizing from a magazine was surprising enough, but two people knowing his name and his business was just plain old odd. He started to feel slightly uncomfortable.

"Wow — how do you two know me?" Brock had to ask. Tonya laughed. She was just as surprised as Brock was. The question she asked herself was, *'How did Luke know who Brock was?'*

"I'm a big yacht fan. I love them. I own a C&B special 2006 limited edition." Luke explained. His eyes were wide and seemed to light up like icicles melting in moonlight.

"You're kidding!" Brock was impressed. Only 3 of those existed in the entire world. They were also very expensive.

Tonya had no idea what a "C&B Special" was other than a model of a boat but she had an idea that if Luke was bragging about having one then it had to be expensive.

The next dance routine started but either of them barely noticed.

"Well this is really something meeting you!" Luke said turning his chair so that he was now part of Brocks table. His hand reached over the table to shake Brock's hand again. It seemed like his whole attitude suddenly changed.

Brock shook his hand and looked over to Tonya. She also turned her chair toward Brock's table.

"And what about you — are you a yacht fan too?" Brock asked her. He was curious what she knew about him.

Tonya felt her cheeks blush like a rose. She was a little embarrassed to say. What could she say other than the truth?

"Ha-ha — no actually, I just saw your face on the cover of some magazine this afternoon. There was a little story about you, and so I read it. I probably wouldn't have even bothered had I not seen you this morning walking past me in the lobby." She confessed.

That was news to Luke. He didn't notice him earlier but that might have been because he was too busy checking out her ass as he followed behind her when they were leaving the GPR earlier.

Brock gave his head a little shake, and chuckled "I must have made an impression on you."

Luke looked between the two. It was so obvious where this was going. *It made him sick to his stomach.* The jealousy inside Luke was now a blazing fire.

Tonya let out a shy laugh. "Well you have a face hard to forget." She felt her cheeks blushing even more.

Brock smiled and said, "I'm flattered."

"It's funny how things work sometimes?" Luke interrupted. "One minute you're on a date with a beautiful woman — the next minute you're watching her fall head over heels for another guy." Luke continued in a sarcastic tone of voice. He silenced Tonya and Brock and made them both feel very uncomfortable. He smirked. Luke enjoyed making them feel uncomfortable and wanted to make them both squirm a little.

Brock and Tonya really had no idea what to say at that moment.

"So how long have you two been dating?" Brock asked as politely as he could, trying to learn something about their relationship.

Tonya laughed. "Oh — we just met this morning."

Luke smirked and said "Yah it's our first date."

Brock chuckled a little, feeling a sigh of relief. *It was only a first date. That meant she was still fair game as far as he was concerned.*

"Well I apologize if I screwed it up a little." He said looking at Luke and then back at Tonya.

"No worries." Luke said in a slow but dishonest tone as he gulped down the last of his drink.

Just then the waitress returned with drinks for the three of them. It was perfect timing.

"So Brock — tell me, how is C&B doing ever since your father died?" Luke asked. The smirk on his face seemed to be growing into a scowl. It was a callous thing to say but he could have been much more callous. He was just getting warmed up.

Brock looked back at Luke. He didn't know what to make of that question. *"Is he mad and taking stabs at me or is he just an asshole?"* He asked himself.

***

"Fine. Everything is just fine." Brock answered in a patient but short tone of voice.

Tonya was wondering the same thing. *'It wasn't the nicest thing to say to someone.'* She wanted to jump in and say something but Luke cut her off.

"I own a lot of shares of C&B you know." Luke said.

Brock raised his brows showing mild interest. There was thick tension starting to fill the air.

"That's great." Brock responded in a short tone again. He didn't like the feeling he was getting off of Luke, like he was leading up to something.

"Yeah—I actually own somewhere near 20% of your stock." Luke paused.

"I'm curious if I should unload or hold out awhile longer. I've been waiting to see what your next design will be like. I mean now that your father is gone—no offence to you—but it makes me wonder if your designs will be of the same caliber."

"What an Asshole!" Brock cursed silently to himself. Again Luke mentioned his father's death. He was starting to lose patience. Also Brock wasn't one for talking business. He didn't really know much about stocks or anything like that. He left all that to his board of directors and the top level execs. What he did know though was that he couldn't discuss anything about the business with a private shareholder. Irregardless of all of that; Luke was really starting to piss him off.

"Listen—Luke—I can't speak business, especially not here, not now, and not with you. Quite frankly I don't even think we should be talking." Brock responded now beginning to show his irritation.

Luke lifted his chin and just stared at Brock for a minute in silence.

Tonya felt the tension rising. It was thick and stifling. If she had a knife she could have carved through it.

———

"Okay guys. It's been fun but I think I should be getting back home now." She said. She didn't want to end the night but she couldn't be around all this tension. The animosity was growing fast. She stood from the table and slung her purse over her shoulder.

Both Luke and Brock watched her stand. Brock made the first move and stood with her.

"Again I'm sorry about tonight Tonya." He apologized with a sincere tone in his voice.

"Oh that's ok... it's not you... I...I'm just very tired now. I had a little too much to drink I think." She responded choosing her words wisely. She wanted to say, "Don't be! It's not your fault, and it's definitely not you I'm upset with" but she thought it was best to keep her mouth shut around Luke right now. After all she was still very aware that Luke had a business arrangement with her mother that wasn't absolutely final. She didn't want to screw that up in any way.

Luke eventually rose to his feet and let out a frustrated sigh. The animosity was pulsing silently between Brock and Luke now. Brock could just sense that Luke was going to say something else to him. *"Whatever he says or does just let it slide — he's not worth it."* Brock kept telling himself.

"I wish I could be as polite as the beautiful miss but I actually value my time." Luke said. His tone was stone-cold serious. His eyes were glued to Brock's and he offered not a single blink of his eye.

"It comes at a high price." Luke explained stopping short, pausing for a second.

Luke wanted to make his next words crystal clear but for Brock's ears only. So he leaned over, so that his mouth was close to Brock's ear and whispered, "I'm sure you can afford it but can you handle it?"

Brock jerked is head away and took a step back. He wanted to punch him right in the face-right then and there. He didn't like being threatened and that sounded and felt like a threat to him. He wasn't quite sure what it meant right off hand but it was creepy and it wasn't anything good.

Tonya reached in her purse and took out her cell phone and called her mother hastily. Luke was getting nastier by the second. Her hand was shaking as she held her cell to her ear and waited for her mother to pick up. Whatever Luke just whispered to Brock, she could tell it upset him.

"Mom?" she asked as her mother picked up the phone.

"Yes dear?" Sandra replied. She could hear the urgency in Tonya's voice.

"Can you come and get me? I'm at the resort still."

"Sure dear, I'll be there in a little bit. Is everything ok?"

"Yes. Everything is fine. I'm just tired and I need to come home — now."

"Ok I'll leave right away. Wait for me in the lobby ok."

"Ok I will." Tonya then ended the call and tucked her cell back into her purse.

Tonya timidly said goodbye to Brock one last time and started walking back inside the resort through the backdoors.

Luke walked closely behind her. He kept an icy glare fixed on Brock until they disappeared back inside the resort.

Brock shook his head. *"Biggest fucking asshole ever!"* He cursed under his breath. He was completely pissed off. "And where the fuck is Quinn and Maria?" He cursed again under his breath. He looked at his watch.

It was 9:45 pm.

∞∞∞∞

Chapter 15

Aboard the Monsters Ball

April 23rd, 2010. 10:00pm CST.

A full moon was glowing high in the Mexican Riviera sky. The Monster's Ball was anchored somewhere in between Cozumel and Playa Del Carmen. There was nothing to be seen outside but darkness, the moon, and its reflection bouncing off the calm watery surface of the ocean. *It was an eerie calm.* Only the sounds of gentle waves softly bumping against the side of the yacht could be heard.

Down below in the gut of The Monsters Ball was a different story. The sound of music could be faintly heard at first from the open concept kitchen and living room area. Then it grew louder further into the back at the top of a small set of stairs that led down into a corridor. The music's bass could be felt thumping. In the hallway at the bottom of the stairs, the music grew louder; still muffled but gradually growing louder none the less. Halfway down the hallway past the first and second bedroom doors on each side — picture frames on the walls were rattling. At the end of the hallway was the master room. The door was shimmying in the door frame from the bass and drums of the music playing.

Another sound could now be heard mixed in with the music. It wasn't the kind of sound that any normal person would make out at first. It was the kind of sound that would have sent chills down someone's spine if they had heard it. It was a sound that most people would hope never to hear. It was the sound of a woman pleading and moaning for it to stop—muffled and gagged. It was the sound of horror and absolute helplessness.

Inside the bedroom was a sight that was even more disturbing than the helpless muffled cries. Inside, Maria was handcuffed to the head board of a king sized bed. She was on her knees and was naked. Tied around her mouth to the back of her head was her thong–it was being used as a gag. The dark mascara she once had penciled around her eyes was smeared down the sides of her cheeks from her tears. Her red lipstick was smeared and smudged around her mouth and chin.

Jacob was pumping his hips violently as he knelt behind her with his big meaty hands gripped tight around her tiny little hips.

Maria's eyes were wide with pain and horror. They agonizingly told the story of the nightmare she was experiencing.

Jacob reached one of his arms far behind his back. He held it there for a second—then brought it down hard; so hard that the palm of his hand rebounded off of one of Maria's butt cheeks. It left a white hot hand print on her skin as the capillaries were momentarily shocked and emptied of blood. Seconds later the white hand print refilled with blood and was now a deep purple, welting print. Maria writhed and a haunting, throaty, agonizing squeal tore out of her throat, only to be muffled by the gag around her mouth.

Jacob reached his other hand up to the back of her head and twisted a fistful of her long, caramel colored hair tightly into his grip. He yanked her head back, so far that the back of her head touched between her shoulder blades. Her throat arched upward. He pushed his hips forward until his pelvis was pressed tight against her bottom. Her squeals intensified and her eyes bulged even wider from the pain and discomfort.

Just off to the side of the bed fastened onto the top of a tripod was a camcorder. It had recorded every minute of Jacob brutally and relentlessly raping Maria. It was going on an hour and a half now of him repeatedly and savagely raping and sodomizing her.

Jacob was getting close to climaxing again for his fourth time since he anchored the Monsters Ball in the middle of the harbor. His hips slammed against her from behind, harder and harder. His voice started to roar and growl as he was building up to his climax.

This would be his last time raping her. He knew the effects of the rufie he spiked her drink with would be wearing off soon enough. *She wouldn't remember a thing.* She would wake up agonizingly sore, and confused, maybe have the odd glimpse of what went on for the past hour and a half, but she wouldn't remember what happened. All she would know is that she was horribly violated and abused.

He still wasn't completely sure what his plan was. He thought about just dumping her off somewhere along the beach; somewhere away from the docks. Whatever happened to her after that was out of his hands. It made no difference to him. There were lots of places he could leave her between the docks and the GPR. That whole beach strip was pretty much a resort haven. He already learned that she was staying at the GPR because of the yellow bracelet she wore around her wrist. It said right on it, Grand Portos Resort. Chances are she'd wake up in an hour or two and try to hobble back there.

He also thought about just getting rid of her all together. He could easily just pop a slug into the back of her head and dump her in the Ocean. He did that many times before and there were enough sharks around to make a quick meal out of her.

A quick thought flashed through his mind about Maria's fiancé. Jacob knew that Maria's fiancé was probably waking back up, and slowly regaining his senses right about now. Even though Jacob found it amusing thinking about Maria's fiancé waking up confused and not knowing what the hell happened — Jacob had a slight worry that there was a possibility the authorities could have been alerted that Maria was missing.

"COME ON!" Jacob growled now thrusting himself rapidly and violently into her tiny body. He had to finish this.

Jacob finished raping her with one final thrust. He gripped her tiny little hips in his large, meaty, hands as hard as he could, and pulled her tight against him. He forced himself as deep as possible inside of her, and climaxed. His voice roared loud as he felt himself pulse and throb inside of her. He was completely satisfied now.

Jacob pulled out of her, stepped off the bed, and shut the camcorder off.

He'd watch it over and over later on. He was certain this was some of his best material yet.

Jacob left Maria cuffed to the bed and whispered, "Shhh… get some sleep now." He watched her collapse face down on the bed even though her wrists were still cuffed to the headboard. She was whimpering and he could tell she was exhausted. He knew that she'd pass out soon–but she'd be lucky to ever open her eyes again. He still hadn't decided on that.

He threw his clothes on, grabbed his Glock19 off of the night table, and shut the bedroom door behind him. He raced up to the deck and into the navigation area of the yacht. He raised the anchor and started the motor and set course back to the PDC marina.

∞∞∞∞

Chapter 16

Quinn comes to

Quinn's eyes blinked rapidly. He felt like someone had just hit him across the head with a telephone book a thousand times. His brain was pounding. The headache was excruciating. He was cold. His body was shivering, almost uncontrollably. His eyes tried to focus but all he could see was a big, blurry, ball of light glowing above him. It took him a second or two to focus and to realize he was looking up at a full moon.

A second later Quinn could hear voices.

They were coming from behind him but they were distant. Quinn's mind was fuzzy and nothing was registering. He could feel himself breathing, he started to take deeper breaths — that was all he could focus on for now. Thoughts and reason were slowly starting to take shape.

"I'm freezing. My head is pounding. I'm taking deep breaths. I'm lying down because I can feel the ground under my back — it's night time because I'm looking at a full moon, and stars are shining. I hear what sounds like wind and water splashing — that's right — I'm near the ocean — I'm in Playa Del Carmen. I can hear voices. They're behind me, maybe 50 feet or so away. I'm starting to remember now. I'm on vacation with Maria — wait... I... I can't remember. Where is she? Where am I? What happened?"

All of these things started entering into Quinn's mind sequentially.

Very slowly Quinn dug his elbows into the sand and raised his upper body and eventually pulled himself up into a sitting position. He felt dizzy, and took few more deep breaths.

"Maria?" Quinn tried calling out to her but his voice was hoarse and faint. It was barely a whisper. He took a minute or two before trying again.

"Maria?" his voice was a notch louder this time. He took a few more deep breaths.

"Maria?" he tried again. His voice was gaining depth and strength — it was coming back now.

"MARIA?" He yelled. It was loud enough that she would have heard him had she been close by.

Quinn rolled himself over onto his hands and knees, and waited a second before he stood up. He was off balance and awkward. He stumbled a few steps backward before gaining his balance. His eyes were squinted as he turned around in a 360 degree circle trying to figure out where he was.

Quinn was on the beach. It stretched into darkness to his left and right. The ocean was dark but glittered with the light of the moon in one direction. In the opposite direction were patio lights, and there was people dancing and moving all around behind a waist high wooden fence. Music was thumping and playing loudly.

"MARIA!" Quinn shouted moving toward the fenced in area. He was still unsteady on his feet and stumbled a few times before getting there. He was swaying to the left and to the right. His balance was slow to return to normal. The only thought on his mind was Maria. He wasn't sure what happened but there was panic forming from deep within his chest and lungs. He could feel his heart beating faster and faster.

Something was wrong–very wrong. When Quinn reached the fence he frantically looked for a gate to open, when he couldn't find it after a few minutes he just climbed over it but fell on the other side. The people close to him thought he was just some guy who obviously had too much to drink. It was nothing new to see someone staggering around, falling down drunk.

It happened all the time.

Quinn pulled himself up hearing the snickers and jests, *"that guy's had too much to drink"* and *"look at how wasted that guy is"* and *"oh my god that guy's tanked!"* but he didn't care about what anyone was saying. It was the furthest thing from his mind. It did however make him question even more what happened but even that didn't concern him right now. He just wanted to know where Maria was.

He just wanted to find her.

Quinn kept looking around for her — scanning the faces and figures in the crowds of people. He pushed past people frantically searching.

"MARIA!" he shouted. She didn't come. People turned to look at him like he was crazy but Maria didn't come. By this time he started replaying the last things he remembered as he continued to push his way through the crowds of people.

They left the resort and found the Blue Manikou just off of 5th Ave. They went inside got a table for two and ordered a couple drinks. Then he actually proposed to her. He remembered he slid his mother's engagement ring down her finger and they kissed. It was perfect and they were both so happy. Then he remembered they ordered dinner. They finished eating — Quinn suddenly tasted the shrimp he ate earlier and it made him dry heave.

Quinn remembered they were finishing their drinks and that they were about to leave, when a waitress came to their table and gave them two complimentary drinks on the house — or so he assumed, because she congratulated them on their engagement. Her English was very broken but that's what he and Maria got out of what she was trying to tell them.

They accepted the drinks and thanked the waitress. That was all he could remember. He couldn't recollect anything past that. He remembered laughing — he couldn't even be sure if it was his laughter, or maybe Maria's or just people around them.

It was all just a blank after that.

After Quinn shouted for Maria a few more times he realized she must not have been in this outside party, he walked inside the back of the Blue Manikou. As soon as he entered, it looked familiar. His bearings were starting to return to normal. He quickly rushed over to the table they were seated at earlier when they were having dinner.

Quinn's balance had returned, he was also thinking more clearly now. His heart however was beating faster than ever. He could just feel in the pit of his stomach that something was terribly wrong.

Amazingly enough underneath the chair Maria had sat in, hidden and tucked into the corner was her black leather, Gucci purse.

Quinn scrambled to pick it up and then he held it tight. The fact that it was Maria's made him cling to it with his life. It wasn't her but it was like a small part of her — it felt like he found a piece of her. He rushed over to the bar counter, there weren't many people around. He rushed up in front of the bar tender.

"Have you seen my girlfrie... my...fiancé?" Quinn
tried asking. His voice was desperate. He didn't know what
else to ask. He could tell the bartender didn't even know who
he was, before he even replied.

"I've never even seen you before. How would I
know?" The bartender replied.
Quinn pointed to the table they were sitting at for dinner.

"We were sitting right over there, for dinner. We had
dinner. A waitress brought us drinks because we just got
engaged." Quinn tried explaining. He could tell the
bartender was trying to remember by the expression on his
face.

The bartender vaguely recalled sending a waitress over
to congratulate a couple on their engagement but couldn't
remember any details.

"I don't remember sorry." The bartender responded.

"The waitress then, is she here? She might remember."
Quinn asked desperately.

The bartender lifted up his chin and scratched at his
stubbly throat for a second trying to remember who the
waitress was he sent over.

"Ah yes. I remember." The bartender said and pointed
to the waitress at the other end of the bar. The bartender
whistled at her to catch her attention. When she looked at
him, he waved her over. The waitress walked over to him and
Quinn. The bartender asked her if she remembered him. He
spoke in Mexican.

"¿Te acuerdas de ese hombre?

She looked at Quinn trying to remember his face but
couldn't be sure. She seen so many faces that night it was
hard for her to remember.

"No puedo estar seguro. ¿Por qué?" She replied also
speaking in Mexican. She shook her head slightly. She said
that she couldn't be sure. And asked why?

The bartender explained to the waitress that Quinn was asking if she remembered bringing him and his fiancé drinks over to their table at dinner and congratulated them on getting engaged.

She remembered now. The waitress remembered how pretty Maria was and how big and beautiful the engagement ring was. She also remembered having to shake Quinn on the shoulder—quite vigorously for a few minutes. That was about 30 minutes after she had given them the drinks and congratulated them.

The waitress also remembered Quinn getting up from the table and stumbling to go outside in the back. She added that she never did see Maria again after she had congratulated them, and that Maria wasn't there when she tried to wake Quinn up. She explained this to the bartender and looked at Quinn.

She could see how worried he was.

The bartender translated what the waitress just told him back to Quinn, and suddenly recalled something as well. He told Quinn that it was some guy that had bought them the drinks and wanted to congratulate them. "I thought he knew you two." He explained apologetically.

Quinn immediately thought that "*the guy*" bartender was talking about, might have been Brock. '*Maybe Brock found where they dining?*' And '*Maybe Maria was with Brock.*'

"What did the guy look like?" Quinn asked. Brock had a very memorable face and striking features. He would know in an instant if it was Brock or not if the bartender described Brock's features—his eyes, or his hair in particular.

"Oh I don't remember—just that he looked like a really strong man." The bartender answered and held his arms out at his sides trying to describe that "*the guy*" had wide shoulders.

92

Quinn did not like the sound of that.

"Like about my size?" Quinn asked motioning at his own body frame. "What color was his hair?" Quinn was desperately hoping that the bartender would describe Brock's features.

"Oh no, much bigger, like a big strong, tough man and I think he had short dark hair." The bartender continued.

Quinn really didn't like the sound of that at all!

"FUCK!" Quinn shouted. Something was seriously messed up with all of this.

"Why? What's wrong sir?" The bartender asked seeing that Quinn was visibly upset.

"She's fucking missing! That's what's fucking wrong! I can't find her!" Quinn shouted in a panic stricken rage.

Both the bartender and the waitress and everyone else around the bar looked at Quinn with widened eyes. They could hear the worry and frantic tone in his voice.

"Did that fucking guy who bought us the drinks touch her?" He asked.

The bartender lifted his hands with his palms stretched outward. He was trying to motion for Quinn to settle down. "I'm sorry sir. I can't be sure. That's all I remember." The bartender replied in a calm, sincere, and empathetic tone.

Quinn was frustrated. He felt his stomach twist into a tight knot. He felt sick. His heart felt heavy. He was angry and worried. He looked at the bartender and at the waitress and could see in their eyes that they empathized with him, it was a fine line between empathy and pity.

"Listen-I'm sorry I yelled. But thank you for your help." Quinn apologized in as calm a voice as he could at the moment. He was shaking he was so upset.

Quinn ran out the front doors of the Blue Manikou. He ran as hard and as fast as he could back up 5th Ave. He was running back to the GPR. He had no idea what time it was but he had to get there and fast. He had to see if Maria was back there.

He started praying to God that she was!

"Please God! Let her be there! Let everything be okay. Let her be safe. PLEASE GOD! I've never asked you for anything in my whole life. I'm just asking this one thing, God. Just let her be safe — just let her be there! I would give everything I have if she's okay. I promise you God. Please let her be there!"

ooooo

Chapter 17

Tonya's flashback

Tonya was standing just inside the lobby doors of the GPR waiting for her mother to arrive. What's taking her? She asked herself. She had only been standing there five minutes but it felt like an eternity. She hadn't felt this uncomfortable since her stepfather Dan Marx had cornered her in her bedroom back when she was 17.

Luke was leaned back against the opposite side of the lobby door, across from her. Tonya tried not to make eye contact with him but she could feel his eyes roaming over her body. Her arms were crossed across her chest and her hands tucked tightly under her arm pits. She felt the need to hold herself tight and protectively.

"How could I have been so wrong?" She questioned herself silently.

Just a few short hours ago Tonya had been thinking he was such a nice, down to earth guy. She even allowed herself earlier in the day to think there might have been a romantic possibility. All through dinner he was charming and polite. Even while they were sitting outside in the back of the GPR he was making her laugh and they were having a relatively good time until Brock Castegere showed up. Luke seemed like the perfect gentleman earlier — *and now he gives me the creeps* she thought. She couldn't even stand to look at him right now. She learned a quick lesson that there was a whole other side to Luke, and it was ugly. He was sinister and downright scary. *"Thank God I found out who he was before it went any further!"* She said to herself breathing a sigh of relief.

The silence was more than awkward. Tonya tightened her arms closer around herself as a chill swept over her body. She didn't know what to say to him. She just wanted him leave. If he said goodnight to her right now — that would have been enough for her to let it go, and thank her lucky stars that it was over but he didn't say a word. He just stood there looking at her. *"Why won't he just leave?"* She asked herself and felt annoyed for being stuck in this awkward situation.

There was clearly nothing left to say at this point. Luke showed his true colors and she wanted nothing to do with him anymore. *The date was over.*

There would be no second chances.

Dan Marx her stepfather flashed through her mind again. It was because she was feeling that same sort of awkward dread that she felt that one day when she was 17 and in her bedroom getting changed. Some unwanted flashbacks started reeling through her mind.

Tonya remembered she had just stepped out of the shower. She wrapped a towel around her body covering her breasts and bottom then sauntered into her bedroom and shut the door behind her. It was a Saturday. It was already bright and sunny out and school had just finished the day before for the summer break. She was 17 years old and just started going steady with a young man named Steven. She was going to meet with him and some friends at the mall, and they were going to spend the day together. She had just taken off her towel when she thought she heard her door creek. Her back was turned to the door so she turned her head to glance over her shoulder. He was standing in her bedroom and he had just shut the door behind him.

Dan Marx her stepfather...

"The Pig!" She snapped — then her thoughts went blank.

Tonya glanced over at Luke with a sneer then looked at the time on her cell phone that she was holding onto tightly in one hand.

It was 10:00 pm.

∞∞∞∞

Chapter 18

Quinn and Brock re-unite

April 23rd, 2010. 10:15pm CST.

Brock finished the last of his corona and stood up from the table. He glanced at his watch again. "This is crazy! Where in the hell are you two?" He cursed to himself. He thought he better go check up at their room again.

This whole night was turning from bad to worse. First he had too much sun. Then he missed dinner. Then he ran into Luke and Tonya which turned out to be a nightmare, and worse than all of that; Quinn and Maria were still nowhere to be found. *"Some shitty vacation this is turning out to be."* Brock scoffed under his breath.

Brock walked back inside the GPR and had to cross back through the lobby to get to the elevator. If they weren't back in their room he wasn't sure what he was going to do. He was just hoping they would be, so that he wouldn't have to keep worrying.

As Brock stepped inside the lobby he noticed Luke and Tonya were standing opposite each other on either side of the Lobby's massive entrance doors. Tonya's arms were crossed and she was staring outside. Luke was staring at her.

Brock didn't want another confrontation so he quickened his pace hoping they wouldn't see him.

Just then Quinn came charging into the lobby from outside. He was running so fast that he slid halfway across the lobby floor as his feet lost traction on the smooth marble flooring. He almost slid right into Brock.

Brock immediately reached out his arms and grasped Quinn by the shoulders, to stop him in his tracks and look him in the face.

"Where the in the hell, have you been?" Brock asked with a big smile. He was glad to see Quinn but still sort of half confused and half angry.

"WHERE IS SHE?" Quinn screamed. His face was beet red and his eyes were bulging and bloodshot. His chest was heaving after having just run as fast as he could from the Blue Manikou.

Brock's expression immediately turned from a big smile into a look of grave concern. He had not ever seen Quinn in such a state before. It scared him. Brock suddenly felt sick to the pit of his stomach.

"Who?" Brock asked. He knew it was Maria that Quinn was talking about but the questions tore out of his mouth anyways

"Maria? Where is she?" Brock questioned.

Quinn grabbed Brock's shirt tightly in his fists and glared into Brock's eyes. It was a look of sheer horror.

"Oh fuck this can't be happening." Quinn moaned.

"What the fuck is going on?" Brock yelled also tightening his grip onto Quinn's shirt in return.
Brock shook Quinn a couple times as he now suddenly was getting this feeling of dread and panic too.

"Some guy at this place. He drugged me. He drugged us. He took Maria. OH GOD THIS CAN'T BE HAPPENING!" Quinn explained in his panic stricken voice.

Tonya immediately ran over to Brock and Quinn unable to help but overhear the panic in their voices. She recognized Quinn from earlier. He was the guy in the boxer briefs who was walking in the lobby in front of Brock. She also remembered the small young woman who had her arm hooked around his. Maria didn't know what happened or what was going but she quickly put two and two together and realized they must have been talking about the girl he was with this morning.

"Is everything okay?" She asked in a concerned voice as she neared them both.

Just off to the side—Listening...

Luke straightened himself out but remained at the doorway. He watched them intently from afar. The moment he heard the words drugged and took her he thought of Jacob. He just sensed something. He didn't know anything about Quinn or this 'Maria' he was talking about, but he knew Jacob—and that had Jacob written all over it.

Brock glanced at Tonya "I don't know!" he said.

"Oh fuck maybe she's upstairs!" Quinn kept swearing and moaning.

"Come on let's go check. Just try and stay calm, we'll figure this all out–I promise." Brock said wrapping one of Quinn's arms around his shoulders. Quinn looked like he was about to faint.

Tonya slipped herself under Quinn's other arm to help Brock support Quinn. Her arm slipped around Quinn's waist. The three of them walked toward the elevator. Quinn started wailing. He was a wreck.

Brock pressed the button for the elevator and it opened immediately. The three of them stepped inside.

Meanwhile...

Luke reached into his pocket and took out his blackberry and quickly sent a text to Jacob as he watched the elevator doors close.

Luke had to check to make sure, so he sent a message to Jacob.

It read "what's going on?"

A few minutes later he received a text back from Jacob.

"Kinda busy. Why?"

Luke didn't like the way that read. He wasn't going to keep messaging—especially not for something like this. He called Jacob's phone.

Jacob answered after 3 rings. "Yah what's up?"

"Were you out tonight?" Luke asked.

"Was—just getting back now." Jacob replied.

"You didn't by chance pick up some company did you?"

"Maybe I did"

"Where is she now?"

"Here—was just going to dump her."

"Don't! I'll be right there."

"Fuck that."

"I said don't!"

There was silence for a moment.

"Somethin' up?" Jacob asked.

"I'm not sure..." Luke replied. He had many thoughts running through his mind. He needed to figure out a few things.

Mainly he needed to learn more about Brock Castegere's life—like who this friend of his was, and who this Maria girl was and more importantly—what they meant to Brock. *Revenge was on his mind.* Tonya was now with Brock which only fed that dark, empty void within Luke with even more reason to want to bring misery into Brock's life.

"Just wait there. I'll be there in 10 or 15 minutes." Luke ended the call and walked casually out of the GPR. He headed for the beach and then started to walk toward the docks to return to the yacht.

The elevator door opened...

Tonya, Quinn, and Brock stepped off the elevator when the doors reopened on the upper level floor. They rushed toward Quinn's room and banged on the door.
"Maria, are you in there?" Brock shouted as he pounded his fist against the door repeatedly. Quinn was frantically trying to feed the key into the lock to unlock the door.

Tonya stood back and tried to clear her head. She didn't know if she should stay or go. She felt like she was intruding but wanted to help anyway she could. She just felt so bad for Quinn. The thought of being drugged and basically kidnapped was just too terrifying to even imagine.

The fact that this was happening felt surreal to Tonya. She would have helped in the same way she did no matter who it was but the palpability of this happening with Brock being in the mix seemed to make it even more surreal to her. She honestly thought she wouldn't have ever seen him again after tonight. Yet here she was with him under horrible circumstances, but with him none the less.

Quinn finally managed to unlock the door and flung it open and rushed inside the room. "NOooo..." He shouted and wailed.

Maria wasn't in the room.

Brock rushed inside after Quinn and looked around frantically and then rushed back outside and quickly unlocked the door to his room.

Maria wasn't there either.

Tonya stepped into the door frame. "Should I call the police or something?" She asked feeling like she should do something.

Brock whipped his head around and looked at her. His heart was thumping hard. He couldn't believe this was happening either. He was worried. He didn't know what to do.

"Yeah—yeah I think that would be best. If you wouldn't mind that would be a great help." He said as he rushed past her and went back inside Quinn's room to be with him.

Tonya stepped out of the door frame and then followed Brock back into Quinn's room. She stopped just inside the door frame, and flipped her cell phone. She realized she had no idea what the number was to the police and 911 would not work here. She called her mother.

"Mom?"

"Hey where are you? I'm in the front of the lobby waiting for you."

"Mom listen, something happened."

"What? Are you ok?"

"I'm fine mom. Don't worry. It's not me."

"Where are you Tonya?"

"Mom, listen..."

"Tonya you're freaking me out!"

"Mom... some people need our help. Can you call the police and send them to the resort? A girl is missing."

"Oh my God Tonya, what's going on?"

"Mom, please... I'm trying to help these people. I just need you to call the police for us. I'll come and meet you in the lobby in a few minutes. Just can you please call the police and wait for me?"

"Ok Tonya... but tell me where you are."

Tonya sighed and looked at the room number on the door.

———

"I'm at room 214. Send them up here ok?"

"Ok dear I'll call them right now."

"Thank you. I'll be down in a bit ok." Tonya ended the call and stepped inside the room with Brock and Quinn letting the door close behind her.

Brock was sitting on the bed beside Quinn. Quinn looked up at Tonya. "Who is she?" He asked Brock. Brock looked up at Tonya.

"Oh...Quinn this is Tonya. Tonya this is my brother Quinn."

Tonya smiled at Quinn. The expression on her face was filled with both concern and sympathy.

Quinn just gave her a quick nod.

"I don't know what to do Brock." Quinn murmured and his head slumped forward until his chin touched his chest.

"Tonya just called the cops — so we'll figure everything out when they get here. Let's start at the beginning though, what the hell happened?"

Quinn sighed and took a deep breath before he explained everything he could about how the evening went down. From dinner, to his waking up on the beach, to his talk with the bartender and the waitress, right up until he ran into the GPR lobby.

Brock and Tonya both listened intently.

They both felt like saying congratulations obviously now that he mentioned that he had just finished proposing to Maria but under the circumstances it might have been best to just say nothing about that.

Neither of them did.

"You woke up on the beach right?" Brock asked, trying to sort out the details.

"Yeah" Quinn replied.

"And Maria wasn't around? Are you sure she wasn't maybe on the beach too, just further away?"

"I'm sure. I looked all around. There was nobody there. And I was calling for her. Besides the waitress said that she wasn't with me when I got up from the table and went outside." Quinn explained sounding utterly frustrated.

"Okay. I'm just making sure." Brock said in a soft voice trying to remain and sound as calm as possible.

"I'm going to call Phil." Brock said.

"Phil who?" Quinn asked.

"Uncle Phil you know — Maria's dad? He'll know what to do."

Quinn nodded and looked at Brock, thinking that was a good idea.

Tonya interrupted in a quiet voice. "What about the lobby? Maybe she left a message or something."

They both looked up at Tonya and nodded their heads.

"Good Idea!" Brock said and reached for the phone immediately. He pressed 0 to reach the lobby front desk.

"Hola, Lobby"

"Hi can you tell me if there were any messages left for rooms 214 and 215, or for Quinn or Brock?"

"Un momento por favor."

There was a moment of silence as Brock was put on hold.

"She's checking now." Brock whispered to Quinn and Tonya looking at them both with hopeful eyes.

"Sorry I don't have any messages for those names or those rooms."

"Ok thank you." Brock said and hung up the phone. He shook his head despairingly "Nothing" he gasped.

"Alright I'm calling Phil now." Brock said, then called the lobby again and asked them to place an overseas call. He knew Phil's number like the back of his hand. He quickly rambled off the numbers and the front desk clerk placed the call for him.

ooooo

Chapter 19

Phil Carter

Phil Carter was Maria's father and an uncle to Brock and Quinn. He was the family and company lawyer and overall go-to-man whenever they needed something.

Phil was a self-made man, and one of New York's top dog lawyers, he was a man with a wealth, and wealth of knowledge and had a never ending list of contacts. If ever Brock or Quinn needed anything, Phil was their contact. He was one of those guys who knew everything, everything, and there wasn't anything he couldn't accomplish.

Phil was 66 years old and had no plans of retiring any time soon. He had grey hair but still looked relatively young. He didn't look like he was anywhere near 66, he looked more like a man in his early 50's. He was in good shape and kept to an active lifestyle.

Phil's day began at 5 am consistently for the past 36 years. He would start his morning off with a hot shower followed by a small healthy breakfast; a bowl of cereal, and a glass of orange juice. Then he'd go for a 2 mile jog around his estate grounds. He had a running trail made especially for this purpose. It was perfectly landscaped with elevated slopes and declines; various terrain types from smooth pavement to gravel parts. *He took his morning jogs seriously.*

After his early morning jog he would take a short 15 minute break and replenish his body with a bottle or two of water. Then he would hit his private tennis court and hit balls for a half hour from his portable 'silent partner' tennis ball machine. When he was finished hitting balls he would eat an orange, and replenish himself with a bottle of Gatorade and have another shower.

Phil always dressed in an expensive Armani suit and perfectly polished black leather shoes. By 6:30am he was ready to go to work. His chauffeur would pull up outside of his estate home in a Rolls Royce and drive him to work to his law practice in one of the Rockefeller centre buildings between 48th and 51st.

Phil spent 99% of the day on the phone with clients and making referrals to one person or another. He finished his day at the office usually by 6:30 pm at which time his chauffeur would usually drive him back home. He would eat dinner and read for awhile and be asleep by no later than 9pm. That was the life of Phil Carter, it rarely changed or wavered from that routine over the past 36 years.

When the phone in his bedroom rang at 11:50 pm EST Phil knew right away something serious had happened. It was a private dedicated line that only a select handful of people had the privilege of knowing the number to. The only time that phone ever rang is if there was a death or a serious accident. The last time it rang was when Henry Castegere died. It was just after 12 am that time.

Phil sat up in his bed removing his sleep mask from over his eyes and reached for the phone.

"Phil here" He said groggily.

"Phil! It's Brock."

"Brock, how are you son?"

A deep sigh could be heard.

"Not good Phil. Not good at all. Something's happened—something terrible."

"Oh God... What happened?" Phil asked.

"It's Maria. She's missing."

"My Maria?" Phil gasped. His voice instantly deepened and became even more serious.

Phil had not seen much of his daughter in the last couple of months. She was living her own life now.

"Yes, Maria. We can't find her and it's a real mess."

"Wait a second. Aren't you in Mexico right now?" Phil asked remembering Maria had left him a message about a week ago telling him that she was going on vacation there.

"Yeah—that's right and we really don't know what to do Phil. We're worried as hell."

Phil was still half asleep but trying to absorb this information as fast as he could. His heart was starting to beat fast and he felt sick to his stomach at the thought of his baby girl being in trouble.

"Okay, listen to me. What happened? I need some details here."

"Ah fuck Phil. You need to talk to Quinn. He can tell you word for word. Hold on a sec." Brock handed Quinn the phone.

Quinn didn't feel much like speaking. He was still in a state of shock but if anyone could help; it would be Phil.

Brock stood from the bed and walked over to Tonya and stood beside her and folded his arms across his chest tucking his hands under each of his arms.

"Thanks for helping Tonya. I'm sorry this is all happening. I just can't believe it, you know." Brock whispered.

Tonya looked at Brock. "Hey don't worry about it. I completely understand. My Gosh, it's terrible. I can't even imagine what you two are going through." She whispered back with an understanding tone.

"Phil?" Quinn asked into the phone.

"Quinn! What's going on? I need to know everything." Phil asked as he fumbled for a notepad and pen he had sitting on his night table beside the phone.

Quinn let out a frustrated sigh. He had to repeat everything again. He didn't want to but he knew he had to.

Phil listened carefully to everything Quinn started telling him. He wrote it down almost word for word. Phil had to ask him to stop a few times and repeat some things for him as he caught up on writing it down. When Quinn was finished, Phil repeated everything back to him.

"That's about it." Quinn confirmed.

"Alright hang tight son. I'm going to make some calls and catch a flight out there as soon as I can."

"Thanks Phil." Quinn whispered.

"Can you put Brock back on the line?"

"Yah sure here he is." Quinn said and handed the phone back to Brock.

Brock reached and took the phone back. "It's Brock."

"Brock, listen I'm going to make some calls, and I'm catching a flight out there as soon as I can. Have you called the Police yet?"

"Yeah they were just called before we called you."

"Okay good. I'll make sure they don't brush this under the carpet. We need to act fast here. So hang tight and take care of Quinn, he sounds messed up."

"He is — and I will. Thanks so much Phil. We'll see you soon then?"

"Yes. I'll be there as soon as I can." Phil hung up the phone and pulled out a large black leather contact book from his night table drawer. It had two thick elastics wrapped around it holding it closed as papers and notes were sticking out from all sides. He flipped through it and found a name and number and started to dial it immediately.

A young female voice answered, "US Embassy Mexico do you know the extension number for the person you are trying to reach?"

"5455" Phil said in a clear voice.

The receptionist who answered patched Phil through to Harvey Duke's home phone.

The phone rang five times before a male voice answered.

"This better be important."

"Harvey. It's Phil Carter here, of Carter & Associates. You remember me I hope."

Harvey Duke suddenly sat upright in his sofa with his back straight and reached for the remote to turn the volume down on the TV.

"Of course Phil, how can I help you?" Harvey's voice turned professional and serious instantaneously.

"I need your help. This is my baby girl we're talking about so it's serious." Phil said gravely.

Harvey stood from the sofa and walked out of his living room and into the kitchen where it was dead quiet.

"My daughter went missing in Playa Del Carmen a few hours ago. Possibly drugged and definitely taken against her will. She just got engaged an hour or so before it happened— so it's no bullshit last night out thing. Remember this is my daughter we're talking about, my own flesh and blood." Phil was blunt and his tone was harsh.

"Okay I understand Phil. What can I do?" Harvey responded.

"I need you to contact the police chief there and explain to him that this is a priority. I want every available officer on this, money is no object. Got that?"

"I understand. Have they been called yet?"

"Yes they've been called to the Grand Portos Resort, no more than 15 minutes ago."

"Okay anything else?"

"Yes. I need you to do some digging. You know find out if this has happened before or if it's just some random thing. Also I need your best guy on this—someone that can get to the bottom of things–fast."

Harvey nodded his head, this was serious business. Phil Carter was a legal giant and when he made a call to anyone for a favor it was because he was owed.

Harvey Duke was no exception. He owed Phil Carter a huge favor.

"I'm on it. There's a guy by the name of Jack Delaney. He's ex special task force, black ops, into real covert, underground type of shit now. We've used him before. He's the best I've seen. Do you want me to contact him?"

"Yes! I'm flying into PDC as soon as I can. Fill him in on what's going on so far and get him on board. I'll contact you as soon as I arrive."

"Got it—I'll get right on it for you."

"Appreciate it." Phil said and ended the call.

Phil flipped a few pages and called another number.

"Hi Bill. It's Phil Carter here. I need a jet ready to go in an hour for Playa Del Carmen."

"Hi Phil, I just got back from there a couple of hours ago. I'll refuel the jet right away." Bill replied.

Phil ended that call and dialed another number.

"Danny! Phil Carter here, I need a car here right away; heading to the airport."

"Yes sir. I'll be there right away."

"Thanks." Phil ended the call and made his way to the shower.

Phil Carter's daily routine was about to be interrupted for the first time in a long time. He was ok with that. This was much more important.

His baby girl was in trouble!

∞∞∞∞

Chapter 20

The cops are called

April 23rd, 2010. 10:50 pm CST.

Sandra Marx had no idea what the number to the police was either. She couldn't understand what was going on but her daughter sounded fine on the phone. She got out of her SUV and walked into the GPR lobby, and headed straight for the front desk. She asked the clerk to call the police for her.

He did—reluctantly.

Sandra was a persuasive woman and usually got her way 9 times out of 10. In the back of her mind she was praying that something had not happened to Luke or something that might foil the chances of the sale going through. She had Luke's signature on the contract but until the property owner signed it—nothing was for sure. She still had to wait until tomorrow for it to be definite and final.

When the police answered Sandra asked them to go to room 214 of the GPR. She explained that there was an incident involving a missing person, with what little details she had been given by her daughter. She wondered if they got a lot of calls like this—*Tourists going missing for a few hours–their spouses getting worried, etc…who knew what happened?* She sure as hell didn't have much to go on, and so it was no surprise the police station clerk didn't seem all that receptive to her call, however he assured her that some officers would be sent over.

The police didn't like interfering at the resorts. It was bad for the tourism business. As a practice, unless someone was dead or missing they usually stayed away. In this case a missing person's report was reason enough to send someone over.

The Mexican government and the effectiveness of their police force didn't need any bad publicity by the press. More often than not a call like this usually ended up being nothing more than a false alarm. Never the less it needed to be investigated. It was better to be safe than sorry.

Sandra gave the phone back to the front desk clerk after being assured by the police that an officer would be there shortly.

Sandra contemplated going up to room 214 to see for herself what was going on but she decided she would give Tonya 10 minutes before re-considering it. In the meantime she would just find herself a place to sit and wait in the lobby.

oooooo

Chapter 21

Tonya stands up to her mother

April 23rd, 2010. 11:00 pm CST.

Tonya felt useless, just standing there watching Brock and Quinn sitting on the edge of the bed. Brock had his arm wrapped around Quinn's shoulders and just kept whispering, "Everything's going to be ok and we're going to get this all figured out."

"Um... Brock?" Tonya quietly interrupted.

"Yes?" He answered and looked up at her.

"Is there anything I can do? Or should I go, or... I don't want to impose..." she asked.

Brock looked at her with a needy look in his eyes. He didn't want her to leave. Her being there somehow felt comforting to him. He didn't want to feel anymore alone than he felt already. He was scared and worried. He was trying not to think of all the bad things that could have happened or what could be happening to Maria at that moment. Tonya being there in the room with them felt right to him.

"I don't know Tonya. I don't mind you being here. If you could stay for just a little while longer I would really appreciate it. But I don't want you to feel like you have to." He explained to her. His voice was shaken. He was trying so hard to be polite, and to sound strong, but really he just wanted to break down. He could feel Quinn shivering. He needed to stay strong for Quinn at least.

"I mean I completely understand if this is all a little too much for you..." Brock said.

Tonya could see how strong he was trying to be and the look in his eyes was so genuine to her that she couldn't just leave. She just felt so out of place, and wanted to do something to help.

"Hey I don't mind being here." Tonya confessed. "Can I get you both anything?" She asked. "How about a tea or a coffee?"

"Quinn do you want anything?" Brock asked quietly.

Quinn just kept shaking and moaning quietly saying Maria's name over and over.

"Maybe a tea might be ok." Brock replied looking up at her with an appreciative smile.

Tonya nodded and smiled back at Brock. "Ok I'm just going to go downstairs to get us all a tea and then I'll come right back. I have to see my mother downstairs too. I'll just be a few minutes ok."

"Ok thank you so much Tonya." Brock thanked her and watched her leave the room.

Tonya left the room and headed straight for the elevator. Her heart was beating rapidly. She felt excited for some reason. Nothing this exciting ever happened in her life before. It was terrible what was happening but at the same time she actually felt like she was part of something bigger than just her usual every day boring life.

When the elevator doors opened up to the lobby, Tonya saw her mother walking toward them. Sandra must have been on her way up to the room. Tonya stepped off the elevator and rushed to her mother.

"You called them right?" Tonya asked immediately.

"Yes. They said they'd send an officer over shortly." Sandra explained.

"Oh thank god."

"Tonya... What in the hell is going on?"

Tonya kept moving, guiding her mother toward the lounge bar. She needed to get three hot teas.
"I'm not even sure mom. It's terrible though. This guy I met — his brother — his brother's girlfriend disappeared!" Tonya tried explaining.

"What? Who? Where? Tonya you're not making any sense."

"Mom, I can't explain it to you right now. I need to get back up there and be with them. I just came down to tell you that I'm fine and that I'll call you later once everything has calmed down ok?" Tonya sighed.

"Is Luke up there with you?" Sandra asked.

Tonya turned her head slowly to look at her mom directly. She had completely forgotten about Luke.

"No... He left — I guess." She replied hesitantly.

"What do you mean you guess?" Sandra asked narrowing her eyes. She was getting frustrated with Tonya's vague responses that seemed to leave her with more questions than answers.

"MOM" Tonya shouted. "Lay off the questions ok! I'll explain everything to you later. I just can't right now. My mind is somewhere else." Tonya's tone was short and snippy.

Sandra's eyes widened. She was taken aback by Tonya's attitude toward her. She was so flustered that she found herself at a loss for words. She was silent for a moment.

"Can I help you miss?" The bartender asked as Tonya stood up to the bar

"Is it possible to get 3 cups of tea to go? I need to take them to room 214." Tonya asked.

"Of course miss." The bartender replied and turned around behind the bar to get her 3 paper cups of hot water and placed a tea bag in each of them.

Tonya reached into her purse and placed a 10 dollar American bill on the bar when he slid them in front of her. The bartender took the bill and slipped it into his pocket. Tonya thought about asking for her change but decided not to as he had already left her corner and was at the opposite of the bar in mere seconds.

She picked up the three hot paper cups of tea holding them tight together, then slowly and carefully started to walk back toward the elevator with them.

Sandra watched her walk past her and then started to follow behind her.

"So what do you want me to do Tonya? Stay up all night and wait for you to call me?" Sandra asked. She was noticeably irked by the tone in her voice.

"No I don't expect you to stay up all night waiting for me to call. Just go home and sleep. I'll be ok. I'll find my own way home." Tonya replied. She felt bad that she snapped at her mother harshly. She couldn't press the button for the elevator to open it either as she stood in front of it. She slowly turned to face her mother again.

"I'm sorry I snapped at you mom. I just don't want you to worry. I'm a big girl now. I promise I'll tell you everything when I get back ok."

Sandra pressed the button for the elevator and it opened right away. Tonya carefully walked back inside the elevator and managed to press the button to go up to the 2nd floor.

∞∞∞∞

Chapter 22

Luke starts planning

April 23rd, 2010. 11:11 pm CST.

"Come on, hurry the fuck up." Jacob growled. His patience was growing thin as he had spent the last half hour or so watching Luke clicking and clacking away on his laptop.

"Shhhh…" Luke hissed. "I'm almost done."

A few moments later…

"She's his cousin!" Luke exclaimed with a proud smile and then twisted his chair around in front the bar counter to look at Jacob.

"Who's, cousin is she?" Jacob questioned.

"Don't you get it? She's the cousin of a billionaire…Brock Castegere."

"You mean to say she's marrying her cousin?" Jacob asked because he had no idea who Brock Castegere was, all he knew is that he saw her having dinner with a guy who was obviously her fiancé.

"No she's not marrying her cousin." Luke groaned. "That guy she was with was Quinn Bailey, and he's Brock's adopted brother. He's also a billionaire!" Luke tried explaining.

Jacob just shrugged his shoulders. He didn't really care but hearing the word billionaire was really the only thing to keep him half interested in what Luke had to say.

120

"What's this mean to me, or us?" Jacob asked. He still wasn't sure why Luke wanted to keep Maria on the yacht.

"Don't you get it?" Luke groaned again. "She's worth a fortune man. Imagine the money they have. Imagine what they would pay for her."

Jacob widened his eyes. Finally what Luke was talking about was starting to make sense to him.

"Oh I get it now. You want to ransom her sweet, little, rich, bitch ass?"

Luke took a moment before answering. His blood was gushing with excitement. His heart was pounding in unison with the wicked thoughts running through his mind.

"The way I see this, is we can play this out two ways." Luke started to explain.

"Oh yah? You see two different ways do ya?" Jacob interrupted. He was trying to be annoying now as pay back to Luke for making him watch him on the laptop for the past half hour.

"Yeah — we can hold her for ransom, and blackmail them with that sick video you made of you fucking the shit out of her. Or we can dump her." Luke responded, un-phased by Jacob's attempt to annoy him.

Jacob was quiet as he listened to Luke. He had creepy smile on his face as he kept rewinding the video he recorded of him raping Maria to certain spot over and over again.

"Well if we keep her. You realize she's going to be my pet right? And you realize that we have to get the fuck out of here? Like now!" Jacob responded to Luke a few moments later. He didn't even bother to look up at Luke. His eyes were glued on the video but he was warming up to the idea of keeping Maria for ransom. His intentions however, were beginning to run wild with even more sick and twisted thoughts of having her all to himself for longer. He was willing to leave it up to Luke though.

Luke had a decision to make. This was treading on new ground. It was risky but either way the excitement of either scenario started to fill that dark empty void inside of him with a new fire. It was perfect either way to him. His petty need to exact revenge on Brock would be satisfied from either scenario.

On the other hand Luke was weighing the risks. He was playing with fire and he knew it. These were billionaires, and their resources would be plenty. 'Could he and Jacob pull this off without getting caught?' Luke wondered. He needed to decide and fast — if they should keep Maria or let her go.

Somewhere in the back of Luke's mind, there was a constant nagging feeling that some day his evil deeds would all catch up with him. Some day, that is — but not yet — it drove him mad trying to shake that feeling and block that ominous thought out from his mind.

Due to that anxiety, Luke rarely did anything without planning it first. He tried to cover all his tracks as best he could for everything he did. He believed that for every action there was a reaction, and as a result he found himself constantly analyzing everything to death.

It became second nature to Luke after awhile. It was almost as though he could foresee the possible futures that would shape his life. He always chose the one that was safest and worked out to his favor. It was different right now. He didn't have that much time to analyze every little detail. He had two possible futures running through his mind. Either they could pull this off. Or they would get caught.

Being caught wasn't an option for either of them. He would die before he got caught. He was pretty sure Jacob would too. It was that very thought that offered him a grim yet hopeful conclusion to all his problems. He had nothing to lose. He cared for nothing except himself and his lifestyle. Death to him was inevitable should he have to choose between living behind bars and losing his lifestyle.

For a long time now, Luke was convinced that the FBI or some other foreign task force agency was on to him and his black market pornographic ring.

Luke didn't trust anyone, sometimes not even himself. He had long since destroyed his credit cards. He had one Cayman Isle., bank account that he kept roughly about half his fortune in. The rest he kept in cash with him on his yacht.

Luke didn't carry any of his real identification on him. He would just keep using passports stolen from random people — because of that, he would keep switching the ownership of his yacht The Monster's Ball to match each passport that he obtained, so that there would be no hassles if he was ever stopped and searched by the coast guard or border patrols. He used only disposable cell phones, because he knew that a subscription service was too easy to track, and that every piece of information relayed was kept on file in big brothers super computers.

Luke applied the same principles to his internet activity. He used only wireless connections, using other people's connections to access the net so that the government www watch dogs couldn't track him.

He hacked into unused domain host servers to host his site from and to provide access to his perverted clients. There were hundreds of thousands of unused domains out there. They were called ghost servers. He developed a program to automatically switch his website from server to server the minute he was shut down or cut off from one. Because of that fact alone it was obvious some authority was watching. Someone wanted him shut down.

Luke went to great measures to conceal who he was, and in the process he often felt he didn't even know who he really was himself. He could be anyone he wanted to be.

There were times however that Luke allowed himself to slide and just be absolutely spontaneous. With his paranoia pushed to the back of his mind he could allow random acts of life to take their course. He had to. It was the only time he felt alive and when he could be his true self.

Luke did it earlier today when he met up with Sandra Marx and her daughter Tonya. He was himself—Luke Cassalon—a wealthy young man investing into real estate looking to make a quick profit, legitimately. He would pay with cash for the property but put the legitimate funds he made from reselling it back into his Cayman Island bank account. That was his 'legit' money. That was his security and in a strange way, his last remnant of decency.

Luke looked at Jacob after he quickly assessed their options. He would work out the details later. He just needed to make a decision right now and go with it.

"Keep her. But here's how it's going to go down. You leave here and sail out somewhere. I'm staying behind. I have to run things close up. I need to see what they're up to, and how they plan to deal with this."

Jacob looked back at Luke. He wondered for a second if he should put so much trust in Luke. On the other hand he'd have the yacht, the girl, and the money. 'Luke wouldn't give all that away and besides Luke knew if he ever crossed him he wouldn't hesitate to kill him.' Jacob reassured himself.

"And then what?" Jacob asked bluntly.

"And then nothing—just wait to hear from me. I'll let you know what's going down and what to do when it does." Luke explained vaguely.

Luke stood up and walked down the hallway and opened the storage room closet. The closet was full of neatly stacked $10,000.00 and $50,000.00 bricks of one hundred and one thousand dollar bills. He pulled out a duffle bag (it was actually more the size of a hockey bag) and filled it up with one and a half million dollars in total. He zipped it back up and walked back to the salon room and picked up his laptop off the bar counter.

"Pass me the camcorder."

Jacob looked at Luke and unplugged the cord from it that ran to the TV. "What do you need it for?" Jacob asked as he slid it down the bar counter toward Luke.

Luke stopped the camcorder from sliding with one hand and quickly flipped open one of the little flaps on the side of it, and took out the SD memory card. He slipped the SD card into his front pocket, and slid the camcorder back down to Jacob.

"You made a back-up of that right?" Luke asked.

Jacob nodded and looked at Luke "Try and keep me up to date every couple of hours, will ya."

"Will do..." Luke responded and climbed the stairs back up to the bridge.

Jacob followed Luke up to the bridge and watched him climb down the ladder and onto the dock.

Luke untied the yacht from the dock and threw the lines back up to Jacob.

"Now get the fuck out of here." Luke shouted.

Jacob smirked and climbed up to the cockpit of the yacht. He raised the anchor and started the engines. The yacht slowly started to drift in reverse backing away from the docks.

Luke glanced over his shoulder and watched the yacht backing away from the docks. He smiled and chuckled to himself as he turned down the beach back toward the GPR.

"This is going to be fun." Luke thought to himself.

∞∞∞

Chapter 23

Luke's dark plan

April 23rd, 2010. 11:30 pm CST.

Four Mexican police officers and one African-American male entered the lobby of the GPR and headed straight for the elevators, just as Luke arrived.

They all waited silently for the elevator to make its way down to the lobby floor from the second floor.

Luke was pretty sure he knew why they were there. He couldn't seem to wipe the smug smirk from his face. He glanced at all five of them, the police officers and the African-American man in civilian clothing. Luke was curious about him. *"Who was he?"* Luke wondered. He could tell he was a physically, powerful man. He had a build similar to Jacob's. *"Ex-Military"* Luke thought to himself *"either that, or some sort of PI."*

The elevator door opened and they all stepped inside.

Luke pressed the number 3 while one of the officers pressed the number 2. The silence was stifling during the short elevator ride up to the second floor. When the doors opened and they all filed out of the elevator, except for Luke. Luke expelled a breath he had been holding. *"Let the games begin boys."* He silently mused to himself.

Luke got out on the 3rd level and made his way toward his room. His room number was 319. As he walked toward his room, he heard the officers knocking on a door on the floor below him. He stopped and glanced over the railing. He looked at the room number behind him, over his shoulder. It was 314. That's all he needed to know to figure out Brock's room was 214.

"Well I know where you guys are at now." He said to himself. He felt like everything was going his way, and he couldn't have been luckier.

A moment later Luke marched over to his own room, unlocked the door and entered. He locked the door behind him and sat down on the bed and opened his laptop. He pressed on the power button and watched as it booted itself up.

The log on screen appeared in seconds. Luke keyed in his password. A black background on his desktop appeared with a few icons and in the very center of his screen was a white circle. He opened his Wi-Fi and Network settings panel. In there he could see a list of available wireless networks in the area. He found the GPR's wireless network and quickly logged on.

Once Luke was connected and online he brought up his command console and began entering a series of commands that would allow him to find the GPR's network administration access points. It was only a matter of time before he hacked into the administration console of their router; and from that point he could have complete control of their network.

Luke could see and monitor what every computer connected to their network was doing. He could even log every keystroke that was made from any computer connected to the GPR's wireless router if he wanted to. He could even hack past their firewalls and gain access to their local network which would allow him full access to the GPR's files and guest registry.

It took Luke 15 minutes to hack his way into their system and gain administrative control. This was the hardest part of his plan and it was easy for him to do, the rest of his plan was going to be a cake walk now. He was preparing for what was to come. He wanted to make sure he had absolute control over the network and the access to view or even control what information was being sent through the network before he moved on to phase 2 of his plan.

Luke reached into his pocket and pulled out the SD memory card he had pulled from Jacob's camera. He shoved it into the SD slot of his laptop and then copied the file onto his hard drive. It was a big file so he began editing it so as to only show a 30 second portion of the recording, a portion in which Maria could be easily identified, as her large engagement ring was clearly visible. He did a little more editing; adding a scrolling marquee at the end of it that read, *"What is she worth to you?"*

Luke chuckled to himself as he saved the file. The next thing he did was some searching. He needed to find Brock's email address. It wasn't hard for him to do. He simply started surfing the C&B website, found a list of contact email addresses and studied the way the company issued emails to employees. It was easy.

Everyone's email was the same. It started with their first name followed by a period, then followed by their last name; so Brock's email would be brock.castegere@cbinc.com. Quinn's was quinn.bailey@cbinc.com. Luke cross referenced the emails to make sure they were in existence by simply typing it into Google.

They both turned up hits under some webpage bulletin that they had both replied to over the past couple of years. It was safe to assume they were still using the same email addresses, but just to be sure; he double referenced it by going to facebook. He created a fake account under the name John Smith and did a search for a friend using their email addresses. A sly grin spread across his face as it brought him to their facebook pages, though their privacy settings were set high, he could still see their picture, and their email addresses.

There was no mistaking that he had their correct email addresses.

The next thing Luke did was find himself a proxy server to mask his IP address. He was going to send an email to them and he wasn't ready just yet for any heat on his trail. He knew that the www watchdogs and even some adept IT people could easily trace the IP address he was using back to the GPR Network, that's why he used a proxy to mask it.

The IP address that would show up as a footprint in the email he was about to send would be completely false, and by the time the authorities obtained a warrant or hacked into the proxy server to find out which IP's were using their proxy this would be all over. Or at least he would be ready for them by then.

Luke started to compose the email. In it he wrote "2 billion dollars and she's yours." then he waited. He didn't attach the 30 second video he edited just yet. He didn't press send just yet either. Instead he lied back on the bed and stared at the ceiling. He needed a little time to think. He knew once he pressed send there was no turning back. There wasn't much chance of turning back now anyways but he needed to try and visualize how all this was going to go down, and how he would pull this off without getting caught.

Luke had to try and see every flaw that might come up and ruin his chances of getting away with this. Once he knew all the flaws, he could easily take measures to prevent them. "For every action there is a reaction." He reminded himself quietly. *"For every positive there is a negative and vice versa."* He continued telling himself.

15 more minutes passed in silence, as Luke lied there and thought of all the things that could go wrong, and how he could prevent them from happening. He began thinking of backup plans for every flaw he could think of. Luke sat up confident that he had a clear enough picture in his mind to go ahead with it.

Luke deleted what he first wrote in the email he was composing to Quinn and Brock and retyped the following message,

"How much is she worth to you? I am guessing she is worth more to me, but this is what we will see. 2 billion dollars and she's yours again. You have 24 hours to deposit the money into the following Cayman Isle account. 3699520118401.

Regards,
The Time Keeper!"

That was the one and only clue he would offer Brock.

Luke remembered full well what he said to Brock earlier that night. He remembered it because he meant it. When he told Brock he valued his time and that it came at a high price he wasn't kidding. All Luke had to do was press *'send'* and it would be game on.

Luke waited with his finger sitting on the enter button. One slight bit of pressure and the email would go directly to Brock and Quinn's email address and then there would be no turning back.

∞∞∞∞

Chapter 24

Jack Delaney

The knock on the door made Brock, Quinn, and Tonya jump. It was a firm knock, and though it was expected, it still made them jump out of their skin.

Quinn hopped up from the bed and jerked open the door. His eyes were puffy and bloodshot, his hair was wild looking and every vein in his body was swollen as his heart pounded with anxiety.

Even at that moment right before he opened the door, Quinn was hoping it was Maria. Instead however the burden in his heart felt even heavier as he saw the police officers and the other man.

Brock stood up and joined Quinn at the door.

"Come inside please." Brock said and opened the door a little wider to let the officers and the other man inside.

Once inside the police officers began questioning all three of them as to the events of their evening. Quinn didn't feel like repeating the whole story again but did so begrudgingly.

The dark man just stood there with his back against the door with his arms crossed not saying a word, but attentively listening to every word that was spoken, and observing everyone carefully in the room.

Quinn rifled through his wallet after he told his story and pulled out a picture of him and Maria and handed it to one of the officers. Brock began telling his story of the night followed by Tonya with hers. The police officers told them all to remain in the room for the time being while they assess the information and get everything moving on this case. They really had nothing to go on other than the Blue Manikou where Maria went missing. They would start there.

The dark man who was silent all this time waited until the police stepped outside of the room and softly closed the door behind them. He took a step forward and looked at Quinn, Brock, and Tonya, with a grave look. He raised a finger to his lips gesturing for silence. Then for the first time he spoke.

"I'm here because I was contacted by a source close to Phil Carter. I'm going to help you guys. I'm going to do everything that can be done to find her."

He held out his hand to Quinn first and introduced himself. "I'm Jack! Jack Delaney." Jack's voice rumbled deeply.

"So what is that you do Jack?" Brock had to ask.

"Let's just say I'm a specialist at this sort of thing. I'm not a cop, I'm not a nice guy; I'll tell you that right now. I do what needs to be done to get the job done. I can't promise you anything other than if there's anything that can be done; I am the one who will make sure it happens."

Jack paused for a moment and looked at them all stoically, "I listened to every word each of you told the police officers, but I can assure you, there are things you haven't told them. It's those things I want to hear. The smallest details are sometimes the biggest clues." Jack stopped for a second and closed his eyes.

"Start from when you first landed at the airport. There's something there. There has to be."

Brock and Quinn glanced at each other and had the same expression on their faces. It was mixed with confusion and deep thought. *Was there something they missed?*

"We got off the plane said thanks and bye to our pilot. We've used him many times and he's been in the company for a long time. Then we met our limo driver. We got in the limo and drove here to the resort." Brock started recounting their day.

"His, name?" Jack asked bluntly.

"Who?" Brock asked a little confused, from being interrupted.

"The limo driver" Jack responded.

"Oh… it was uh..."

"Miguel" Quinn interrupted.

"Why does that matter?" Brock asked curiously.

"Trust me it matters. You didn't tell the police any of these things — remember it's the small details that I'm looking for." Jack explained.

"What happened next?" Jack asked urging Brock to continue on.

"Nothing, he parked in front of the resort, and let us out. He got our bags out of the trunk, and I tipped him, shook hands and that's it." Brock explained.

"Wait… Brock, that's not all." Quinn interrupted again. "He took a picture of us right before that, remember?"

Brock nodded his head. "Oh yah… that's right. He snapped a picture of us, right before we went inside."

Jacks eyes flashed open and looked at Quinn with a curious squint. "That struck you as odd, didn't it?" Jack asked curiously.

Quinn thought about it for a second and realized that he did find it odd-now that he thought about it.

"Yeah, I don't know why but it just made me wonder."

Jack nodded knowingly. "That's because your gut first told you that it was strange-Not normal-out of the ordinary in some way, right?"

"Y… Yeah I suppose I did find it a little strange. It made me wonder, but I passed it off as maybe he took pictures of all his clients?" Quinn responded.

Brock's eyes furrowed, he had to admit that he found it odd himself for just that first split second, but like Quinn just explained, he passed it off with the same thought–That Miguel probably took pictures of everyone he chauffeured.

"Did you see him again after he dropped you guys off?" Jack probed deeper.

"No." Brock said quickly.

"Wait–Maria and I saw him again; he was outside the Blue Manikou; that's one of the reasons why we went in there in the first place. We waved at each other." Quinn explained. His voice was starting to rise with suspicion and he was talking faster now.

"You don't think that little fucker had something to do with this?" Quinn asked feeling his anger rising.

Jack looked at Quinn stoically and said nothing for a few seconds. "I'm not sure yet Quinn. I can tell you though that in most cases like these, it's usually someone who had somewhat close contact. You're in a different country and this sort of thing happens a lot here. More than you know. These kinds of people are like predators, and when they see something they like, they go after it."

Quinn looked even more upset than before and a storm of memories flashed through his mind like a slide show. Quinn remembered that Maria took Miguel Sanchez's card out of the back of the limousine while they were driving to the GPR and slipped it into her purse.

Quinn suddenly rifled through her purse quickly and frantically. He pulled Miguel's business card out and held it shakily in his hand.

Jack narrowed his eyes and leaned forward to take the card from Quinn. He studied it for a moment before slipping it into the chest pocket of his shirt.

"Is there anything else odd or not sitting quite right?" Jack asked calmly.

Quinn was shaking again. He just shook his head unable to think of anything else at the moment.
Brock stirred a little. There was something sitting uncomfortable with him all right, but he was sure it couldn't be connected to what happened in any way. After all… *how could it be?* He looked at Tonya for a second, then up at Jack. "Well…" He started. "I know this is probably nothing, but if it's anything then maybe you'll know."

Jack nodded urging Brock to continue.

"Well… just earlier, when Tonya and I first met. The uh… guy she was with. It's been bugging me ever since. He was hostile, very threatening toward me, and he said some things to me that just seemed to be way out there. I can't explain it but my gut just tells me something was seriously wrong with him — but this would have been all at the same time with what had already happened with Quinn and Maria."

Jack nodded his head slowly as he looked at Brock then at Tonya, then back at Brock. "I need only a name."

Tonya's eyes widened a little. She felt uneasy.

There was no way Luke was connected with this. She had been with him throughout most of the day; at dinner, and later that evening. It was impossible.
"I don't think so." Tonya spoke up, her voice cracked. *There was no question there was something wrong with Luke but there is no way he could have had anything to do with this.* She thought to herself.
"I need his name please?" Jack asked again.

"Luke…" Tonya answered meekly. She didn't really want to bring Luke into this, and was afraid to say his last name even though she was having a hard time remembering it right now anyways. She felt bad but more gut wrenching worried that now she might screw things up with her mother's sale.

"If he has nothing to do with this, then he's safe." Jack assured her sensing her doubt and uneasiness about the whole thing.

"Well I just don't think that Luke could have anything to do with it." Tonya said again.

Jack looked at Tonya for a moment in sheer silence, studying her. She didn't give him a last name–Why?

Tonya could feel his eyes burrowing into her. He was intimidating, and it made her feel extremely awkward. She wasn't by any means trying to defend Luke but she just whole heartily believed there was no way Luke was involved.

"Why? What makes you so sure he has nothing to do with this?" Jack asked in his deep rumbling voice.

"I … I just think that because I was with him most of the day, and throughout dinner, and later this evening, and that there's no way he could have anything to do with it. That and the fact he didn't even know who Brock was." Tonya explained turning to look at Brock for reassurance.

Brock looked at Tonya and nodded. "Yeah… that's true. He didn't know who I was at first."

"Look I know there was something not right about him. I felt it and noticed it too, but I think it was just pure anger and jealousy if anything." Tonya continued glancing back at Jack.

Jack narrowed his eyes slightly. "I'm not saying he had anything to do with it per se, I'm just trying to get you all to understand that I look for irregularities, and things that don't seem right. It's those things that usually hit you in the gut. It's your intuition telling you that something isn't right or is out of place. In my experience, 99% of the time it's those very irregularities that are the biggest pieces to the puzzle. They usually hold most of the answers. For instance, I can tell that even though you might truly believe he had nothing to do with it, there's something more. Something you're keeping to yourself about this Luke fellow."

Tonya felt her cheeks and forehead start to heat up. She was keeping the fact that she was also worried that if they started snooping around into Luke's life, and he somehow found out, he would freak out and ultimately screw up the big sale with her mother.

"Well I'm just worried if you start snooping around into Luke and he finds out it will mess everything up for my mom so bad, and I also don't believe he had anything to do with this– he was just jealous." Tonya blurted out feeling now defensive but being utterly honest.

"And you know he was jealous because you and Brock, were sharing a common attraction for one another while you were on a date with this Luke fellow." Jack concluded.

Both Tonya and Brock looked uncomfortable and were at a loss for words.

"Look I don't see why any of that matters. You asked if there was anything that didn't sit well with me and I told you." Brock said raising his voice slightly.

Jack just looked at Brock unassumingly. He wouldn't push anymore about this Luke fellow.

"I'm just trying to help you all understand what I look for. It's my job–It's what I do–I see things in a way that most people don't, and if I can see enough, then I can help you get to the bottom of what happened. Listen. We have a lot to go on so far. We have a couple names. We have a place where it happened. We even have a couple witnesses. All we need now is to make sure that we have enough of the pieces of the puzzle so that I can start piecing it all back together and find out what happened to Maria, and with any luck get her back safely."

Quinn's sobbing filled the room again upon hearing those words. "She's gone isn't she?" He asked looking up at Jack.

"Listen to me Quinn." Jack whispered. Quinn's sobbing was starting to irritate him but he was empathetic enough to understand.

Jack looked Quinn directly in the eyes and quietly said, "I know this is rough. It's a horrible thing, but I need you to be strong. I need you to be a man, and instead of sobbing there like a child, you need to brush yourself off and be strong for her. She needs you now more than ever before. Your crying isn't going to help her–but your mind can! You have to think now, think deep and hard to remember. If you can remember anything; ANYTHING at all when you were at the table having dinner–before it's all a blank, or even sometime in between, or when it's fuzzy, it will help her. Now take a deep breath gather yourself and try, try for her Quinn!"

Quinn nodded and wiped his eyes. He practiced breathing. He took in a few deep breaths and felt himself calming down. He was thinking of her, he was thinking of helping her. He wanted to be strong for her. He was her man.

"Ok… Ok I can do this for her." Quinn said quietly feeling a sense of strength building inside of him. Just thinking of Maria's smile, and how she looked at him, and how he wanted to protect her always–it gave him strength. The way he felt when he was with her. The way he wanted to treat her–like she was a queen. It made him feel connected. It empowered him with a deep inner strength.

Quinn started by focusing on their dinner at the Blue Manikou. He proposed to her. It was perfect. They were so happy. A waitress offered them drinks that were paid for. They toasted. They started talking about when the big day should be. They were setting a date–In one year exactly from today's date. They were laughing. They were so happy. They were excited but then–*tired*–this extremely tired feeling came over him. *He was so tired*. And then… that's it… someone sat down at their table across from him and beside Maria. They shook hands–Jack… "JACK!" Quinn shouted in a growling voice. "His name was JACK!"

Jack's eyes flinched just for a second hearing his name being said with such anger. "You remember him?" Jack asked leaning forward close to Quinn again.

"… His face is so fuzzy but he's a white guy. He looks pretty big. He had a real creepy laugh too. He's American. I can tell by how he sounded. And oh fuck I can't make out his face–Fuck I want to kill him." Quinn was voice was an angry growl and he was grinding his teeth. He couldn't make out his face but he could see him. He heard him. He was so close to him. He even shook his hand. Quinn's anger was raging.

"You did good Quinn. You did damned good." Jack said placing a hand on his shoulder reassuringly. "We're getting close to him now. Really close. You shook his hand? He told you his name–anything else? Is there anything else at all?"

Quinn squeezed his eyes shut tight and tried to remember.

"Wait… something about–he wants to party–he has a place–No a boat! He has a boat… not far…" Quinn was saying.

"He's at the docks!" Jack blurted out loud interrupting Quinn. Jack now put both hands on Quinn's shoulders. "You did good Quinn. He's at the docks. You all stay here." Jack said in a quiet voice before he stood up straight and swung open the door and quickly tore out of the room.

Quinn, Brock, and Tonya were in a state of shock. They didn't know what just happened as it happened so fast. However for the first time in hours, it seemed like something was finally going right. *They were close.* They could feel something changing, like hope was returning quickly, and this might be all over soon.

∞∞∞∞

Chapter 25

A storm was brewing

April 24th, 2010. 2:00 am EST.

It was raining. There was thunder and lightning. It was dark and dreary. The stars in the evening sky were hardly visible through the heavy night time clouds.

There was more than one storm brewing this night, as Phil Carter was feeling the storm inside himself raging just as much as the storm he was experiencing outside right now. His driver drove onto the runway tarmac as close to the small private jet as possible.

There it was the same Honda HA-420 jet that Brock, Quinn, and Maria arrived in at Playa Del Carmen early yesterday. Standing just beside it was Bill Creston, the long time C&B Inc. company pilot, the same pilot that flew Brock, Quinn, and Maria into PDC yesterday.

Bill Creston was holding a large black umbrella shielding himself from the downpour of rain in one hand, and a cup of Timmy's large double-double coffee in the other hand. The wind was clearly blowing face on as his long overcoat was flapping behind his back and was pressed tightly to his chest.

Phil looked at him through the rain streaked window from the backseat of the Mercedes Benz for a moment, while his chauffeur put the car in park and got out to retrieve Phil's suitcase and umbrella. The chauffeur rolled his suitcase over to Bill and shook his hand, then turned back toward the car to open the door for Phil after carefully opening the umbrella. Phil stepped out of the back as the chauffeur leaned over offering the shield of the umbrella. They walked side by side back over toward Bill. They shook hands.

"Good to see you sir! Some fine weather we're having tonight huh?" Bill joked.

Phil smirked. "Yes wonderful... just wonderful."

Phil shook hands with his chauffeur and gave him a quick nod, and with that the chauffeur quickly trotted back to the car, braving the rain, as he left Phil holding the umbrella.

"I'm sorry for the short notice Bill." Phil started.

"No need Mr. Carter. I'm always available for you." Bill responded with a humble smile. "Shall we get out the rain?"

"Please!" Phil replied quickly.

A few moments passed as they climbed into the jet and settled in taking off their jackets. Bill fired up the engines and let the jet idle and warm.

Phil settled into the co-pilots seat beside Bill and after a couple of brief moments as Bill checked all the gauges they looked at each other.

"So here's the situation. I had to register our flight plan and because of this storm right now, there were some delays. But all is good. We can commence our flight at exactly 2:10 am, which is in just a few minutes." Bill explained in his professional pilot like tone.

Phil nodded and offered a small nervous but appreciative smile.

"So… are we going to be ok with this storm and all?" Phil asked with a small element of concern in his voice. He really didn't like flying that much, let alone in the small jet in the middle of a night time storm.

Bill laughed, "Well I'm not going to lie to you and tell you it's going to be a smooth flight. It's going to get bumpy and choppy as hell up there, but the good news, is that this storm is only blanketing the tri-state area and we should be out of it within a half hour. After that, it should be a smooth comfortable flight." He explained.

Phil nodded and said, "Well I guess a half hour of nerves isn't so bad."

"That's the spirit!" Bill said with a broad smile. "Well buckle yourself up, get cozy, and we'll get on our way." Bill said as he strapped himself into position in the pilots chair and started performing the gauges and engine diagnostics check once again.

When everything was good to go, Bill revved the engines and steered the jet down the runway to get into position for take off.

Once in position they remained idle for a moment while Bill verified with the tower that he was clear for take off. He was given the green light after 30 seconds, and with that the jet began to speed down the runway.

The engines roared and the small jet screamed down the runway, the nose began to lift. **10 seconds, 9 seconds**–it lifted higher. **8 seconds**–of runway remaining. Lightning split the sky and cracked like a whip followed by a roll of thunderous booms. **7 seconds**–the nose was in full tilt and the feeling of weightlessness beginning to take over could be felt. **6 seconds**–the jet began to lift just less than an inch from the smooth pavement of the runway. **5 seconds**–another streak of lightning split the sky like a jagged fork, followed by an angry crackle and hissing sound. **4 seconds**–the engines were screaming at full throttle, and the jet was lifting now an inch above the runway, its nose arching a little more upward, pointing to the sky. **3 seconds**–beads of cold sweat started to form on Phil's forehead; his knuckles were turning white as he gripped the arms of the co-pilot chair he was seated in. He could see the runway running out and the dismal green of the grass field that carried on after it. *"FUCK I hate flying!"* Phil cursed silently to himself. **2 seconds**–a gust of air swept beneath the jet and shoved it to the left a little. 1 second–the nose was over the grass — Bill was pulling back on the steering yoke with a strained expression on his face. **And lift off**... They were 12 inches above the grass field and maintaining steady elevation.

They made it.

Phil let out a deep sigh of relief. In minutes they were at safe flight elevations and streaking across the night sky.

∞∞∞∞

Chapter 26

Maria Awakens

Maria couldn't feel her arms. They were numb, and her shoulders felt like they had been torn out of their sockets. Her head was spinning and as she opened her eyes trying to gather her senses, everything was blurry and spinning like a whirlwind. She was disoriented and extremely confused. Second by second her senses started coming back. She could start to feel different parts of her body. First her toes, then her feet, then her legs, then her bottom and pelvic area.

'Something wasn't right' — Maria felt naked and sore, and violated. She was laying face down and she lifted her head slightly, still unable to feel or move her arms. As she lifted her head she tried rising up on her knees, and did so for a second, only to collapse face down on the bed again.

Her heart started beating faster — 'something was seriously wrong.' Maria attempted to rise again. Her eyes were still blurry but clearing slowly. Things were beginning to come into focus slowly. She was in agony her shoulders more so than any other part of her at the moment. She blinked rapidly trying to focus on her arms. They were stretched out in front of her but she couldn't feel them.

Maria tried moving her fingers but there was nothing. She lifted her head more to get a look at was wrong and why she couldn't feel her hands and arms. Her heart sped up as a rush of panic came over her from what she was seeing. Her hands were in handcuffs and looked purple. They were cuffed to the head board high above her head and obviously the blood hadn't been able to circulate for god knows how long.

Maria suddenly realized she was in trouble. She was naked, and she was handcuffed to a headboard on someone's bed. Something was tied around her mouth used as a gag. She immediately attempted to rise up to her knees and ultimately up on her feet, trying to stand so that the blood would drain back down into her hands. "Oh God..." She gasped which was muffled by the gag tied around her mouth. She was terrified. Even If she wanted to scream she couldn't. She wasn't sure if that would have been a good idea to anyways.

It didn't take Maria long to realize she had already been raped and brutally violated. She felt it—everywhere. She felt disgusted and sore and just wanted to crawl out of her skin but all that was quickly stored into the back of her mind. She was starting to panic. Her heart was racing hard and fast. She was starting to hyper ventilate as she tried to wriggle free from the cuffs with no luck.

She was trapped...

Maria swung her head around from side to side taking note of the room she was in. She was standing on a king sized bed. There was a tripod beside it. An end table, a dresser, an armoire, and a big widescreen LCD TV mounted on the wall.

The door was shut. Off to one side there was small archway and what looked like a couple of stairs that led downward. There were two small sealed rectangular windows on each side of the room as well. She couldn't see anything outside. It just looked black.

Maria kept struggling trying to free herself from the cuffs. Her arms were like noodles, and she could feel the blood rushing back down them and into her hands as the pins and needles sensation made her almost scream out loud. It was painful and agonizing but her fear of what was beyond that door or down those couple of steps was stronger than the pain.

She realized there was no way the cuffs were coming off her wrists. That's when she took a moment and took a few deep breaths to try and calm down. She started thinking clearly again. She was inspecting the headboard. If she could somehow get the cuffs off the headboard, at least then she could get off the bed and move around. She struggled from one side to the other trying to shimmy them off the rung of the headboard, but the corner posts were blocking her efforts.

She couldn't get free.

Her hope was fading fast, but her desperation was growing by the second — and like a miracle, out of the corner of her eye, sitting right there in front of her eyes on the night table was one single little key. It had to be the key to the cuffs.

It just had to be…

∞∞∞∞

Chapter 27

On the docks

Jack met the four Mexican police officers outside the room. One was busy filing the missing persons report over his two way radio while the other three were discussing something in their native tongue.

"Come on, we're going to the docks. Put out an APB to all available units to meet us there." Jack said as he hurried past them. He spoke fast and made it clear he was in charge.

The cops were already told by their chief of police before they left the station with Jack that he was in charge. None of them knew who he was but thought he must have been some big shot FBI agent or something. It was very rare they let foreigners into their policing circle, and even more rare, to let them call the shots. The only explanation was that this missing girl must have been someone very special, and knew someone with very deep pockets.

Jack and the cops all hurried to the elevator and filed into it. The officers were calling in the APB for all available units to converge on the marina. In minutes Jack and the officers were in their patrol cars and screaming down the streets of Playa Del Carmen. Other police cars were racing toward it as well. The howl of sirens filled the streets and the flashing lights lit up the town like a disco.

It took only a couple of minutes to get there. Other police arrived moments later, and it didn't stop there. There had to be at least ten cars and a squadron of cops all jumping out, gearing up and getting ready bust some doors down.
 This was high priority and a service not usually granted for a single missing girl. It had only been a couple hours after all – but with the right connections–*people jumped*– they not only jumped but they asked *"how high?"*

It started with the call from Phil Carter to Harvey Duke; then from Harvey Duke to Jack Delaney; from Jack to Mario Santoro (the minister of justice); from Santoro to the chief of police, and so on, it made things happen–*fast*. The key words *"Money was no object"* from Phil Carter's mouth was the icing on the cake. Everyone would be going home with a big fat bonus when this was all said and done.

Jack pulled a Kevlar out of the backseat of one the squad cars and checked his desert eagle service issued gun making sure the clip was full. Click, clack, click, the noises of officers loading ammo and readying their guns filled the lot in front of docks.

"Let's do it!" Jack yelled out confident everyone was ready. *He knew he was.* The search was on. Jack and the squadron of cops converged onto the 4 long docks in groups of five on each one. The flash light beams were everywhere as they tactically crept down the docks. At each boat that was docked three officers would board the boats while two stayed watch on the dock beside it. One by one the search continued. People were ordered out of their boats, while each boat was thoroughly searched and ransacked. It took close to an hour and a half by the time Jack called off the search and regrouped the entire squadron. Almost every person who did happen to be in their boats became subjects of interrogation.

They didn't get much out of anyone. Yet there were a few leads. Several people did mention that there was a really big expensive looking yacht that pulled out earlier. It came back then left again just a couple hours ago. There was nothing suspicious about it other than the fact that it came back and left in the dead of night which was unusual.

There was one person of particular interest that the squadron of police, cuffed and were holding. His name was David Carnes. He was in his early twenties, clean cut looking guy, average build, quite average looking, of American descent. He spoke English and was at the moment shaking and scared as hell.

During the raid, one of the teams found a substantial amount of marijuana in his small sail boat. He was a small time trafficker no doubt. Probably had his own little enterprise of running the marijuana from PDC and Cancun, back into Florida. A find like this with a couple of kilo's of marijuana he'd be serving the rest of his life pretty much behind bars in a hardcore Mexican prison. It would be a terrifying thought to any young American to be sure.

Jack walked over to the trembling young man. He asked the officers first what was going on. They explained the situation quickly, and Jack just nodded his head. He looked at the boy sternly and shook his head with a look of pity on his face.

"It's such a shame, a young guy like you throwing your life away, and for what? Some easy cash so you don't have to go out and get a real job? It makes my stomach turn kid. It really does." Jack drilled into him.
David looked up at Jack with worry in his eyes.

"How did you guys know?" David asked.

Jack's eyes widened just slightly before narrowing down into David's.

"That's it huh? No apologies, no regrets, just baffled as to how you got caught?" Jack responded.

David looked down at his shoes and just shrugged his shoulders.

"We didn't know. This wasn't about you. You're not important enough to have had this come down on you. You're just a piece of shit with no luck tonight kid." Jack laid into him.

David looked back up at Jack surprised and confused.

"It's not?" David asked in a shaky voice.
"We were looking for someone of significance. Someone who's on a very big boat actually — so unless you know something about that–you can just sit there and enjoy the air while you can, because kid, you're going away to some little stinking shit hole cage with a bunch of sweaty Mexican's who are probably hungry for some young white American ass." Jack said gravely.
David's eyes widened a little with a flash of both fear and desperation inside them.
"And if I do know something? What will that get me?" David asked, recognizing a possibility of hope of being let go.

Jack glared at him with an icy cold stare.

"Then you got about 30 seconds to spill it, or it's off to that sweaty little hole I was talking about."
"But will you let me go?" David asked desperately.
"Spill it." Jack snapped demandingly.
"The Monsters Ball, that's the name of that big yacht that was here. I saw this one big guy carrying a girl inside earlier–over his fucking shoulder man. It was fucking creepy as hell. That's all I know" David confessed what he knew.
Jack nodded his head. He hid a smile that was about to stretch across his face. This was a huge lead.

"You did good kid." Jack said. "But what gets me is that you saw something like that and you did nothing? Why? I'll tell you why, because you're a coward and a little flea bag. You were too selfish — it's always all about you isn't it? Even though you knew that girl was going to be in trouble, you were too selfish to even pick up the phone and try and help her." Jack said with a sneer and tone of disgust.

After having said that, Jack turned his back to him and simply walked away. He had what he needed, but the kid had to learn his lesson. He would never learn otherwise.

"Can I go?" David yelled out, confused as to what was going on.

Jack kept walking and just slowly shook his head side to side. *"Not a chance!"* he muttered under his breath.

The cops grabbed David and roughly stuffed him into the backseat of one of the squad cars and slammed the door.

"WAIT!!!" David's voice turned desperate. "LET ME THE FUCK OUT!!!" It was a familiar scene — *First the swearing,* "YOU FUCKING LIED TO ME!!!" *then the anger*- followed by a tantrum of head bashing against the window. The frustration of knowing there was nowhere to go now. "I'LL FUCKING KILL ALL OF YOU!!!" *The empty threats started spewing* — more head bashing against the window. A couple minutes and a headache later, he was now starting to realize that no one was paying attention-*no one gave a shit.* "COME ON PLEASE!!!" everything he yells as he looks out the window desperately trying to make eye contact with someone, is soon met by a moment of silence. *That moment of realization* — "PLEASE!!!" — When it becomes **REAL** — *He's fucked now.* He's going to that dark sweaty hole of a cage that Jack was talking about. He was sure to be raped, and spend God only knows how long, wishing he never got caught. His freedom lost and about to learn just how miserable life can be.

∞∞∞∞

Chapter 28

A change of plans

Luke's finger was still tapping on the enter key on his laptop. His heart kept spiking with adrenalin, just when he thought he had the nerve to press it — he froze.

There were loose ends Luke couldn't quite figure out how to correct. No matter how much he wanted to push them to the back of his mind, to that place where insignificant things are stored, he couldn't.

Luke was much too paranoid and cautious to do that. This was a whole new ball game. This was big time crime. This was kidnapping, extortion, bribery, unlawful confinement, accomplice to rape, assault, etc... the list of charges he'd be nailed with would quite literally be endless.

If this didn't work out in his favor, he'd be spending the rest of his life behind bars. That to Luke was worse than death. He would go insane and kill himself if it ever came to that. Yet the very thought of committing suicide didn't sit well with him. There was an element of doubt within that whispered he wouldn't be capable of it. He was far too self absorbed to hurt himself. Instead he could visualize himself going down in a blaze of gunfire, taking down as many other people with him as he could. That was the ideal fantasy in his mind.

Luke took one more deep breath and exhaled slowly. His finger shifted from the enter key to the backspace key. He moved the cursor to the end of the body of the email, and slowly pressed down. The cursor began erasing all of what he wrote. He then removed the video attachment and deleted who the email addresses and logged out.

There were two too many loose ends. No matter how he looked at it there was no getting Sandra and the whole real estate transaction out of the way. He had to meet with Sandra tomorrow. There was a paper trail. His real name, the real Luke Cassalon, the one who was legitimate and investing into a real estate contract was locked into an agreement. There was no way out of it unless the owner of that property decided to refuse his offer. The chances of that were slim to none. It was a million and a half cold hard cash and Luke was pretty sure that there was no way the guy would refuse it.

The fact that there was a paper trail in the middle of all of this, if he were to have sent that email, was just too big of a risk for Luke. He wasn't willing to chance it. He thought he was, but in the end his instincts prevailed. If he was sure his evil scheme would have worked, he would have pressed that enter button without hesitation and sent the email but he couldn't be sure.

There was also his jealousy. He couldn't get Tonya out of his head. He actually felt like a good decent person with her — up until Brock interfered with their night. Maybe that was why he was so enraged with jealousy and hell bent on revenge? Maybe it was because he caught a glimpse of what the "good" Luke Cassalon could have been like. He was charming. He was polite, he felt like he wanted to make her happy; but because of Brock that rare hopeful glimpse, was quickly washed away.

Tonya was with Brock this very moment. He was sure of it. He watched her leave with him, helping walk Quinn into the elevator.

"It wasn't meant to be. Not this day, and not this way." Luke was thinking to himself. "But this is far from over. One day—and when you least expect it, I will ruin your world Brock Castegere. Mark my words. Little by little I will take everything you have away from you, and I'll make it mine, and I'll make your life a living hell! "Luke's thoughts were darker and more disturbing than ever.

Unimaginable schemes were already twisting through his mind like a cyclone. If it took him days, weeks, months, or even years, he would have his revenge—and when he was ready, you could be sure his plan would be thought out to the extreme of perfection. There would be no loose ends, and nothing standing in his way from exacting his revenge on Brock Castegere.

Luke logged back into his email and typed Jacobs email address in the bar. For the subject he typed, "COP". That was the word. It meant (Change of Plans). It also meant abort. In the body of the email he proceeded to type a short message,

"I'll be in Cancun tomorrow. Meet me there ok. Leave now! PS. Bring your lady friend… or not. Doesn't matter, just don't leave her here. The heat is too much!"

Luke moved his cursor to the send button and pressed the enter key. The email was sent. Jacob would receive it in a minute or two. He logged out of his email and then pulled the SD card out of his lap top. He erased and shredded the video file that was on his hard drive.

Luke's message to Jacob was somewhat cryptic because he couldn't very well say anything that might be incriminating, yet it was simple enough that Jacob would easily know what to do. He didn't feel worried.

For now he was tired of thinking, and just wanted the night to end. It was a long day and though it was still relatively early, it felt like an even longer night.

Luke disconnected from the GPR'S network. No one would even know he was on it, or that he had hacked into their system.

He left no traces.

After making sure all his tracks were covered, he closed his lap top and eased himself down on the bed lying on his back. His head sank comfortably into the pillow, his eyes closed and in minutes he was asleep.

∞∞∞∞

Chapter 29

Struck by lightning

"Mayday, mayday, mayday — this is flight Charlie Bravo 1 2 9, we're going down... requesting emergency assistance. Emergency broadcast beacons are activated. I repeat emergency broadcast beacons are activated." Bill Creston repeated into the MIC on his headset for the third time. He spoke fast yet sounded incredibly calm despite the situation.

The wind was hissing and blowing in a furious rage. Rain was spraying into his face as he was trying to pull the steering yoke higher, desperately trying to maintain control of the jet.

The cockpit window was cracked and the cracks were spreading out like a spider's web. The system warning lights and alarms on all the gauges in the cockpit were beeping and ringing, and flashing out of control. The engine on the left wing was spewing out a trail of sparks, and flames, and the sounds of grinding metal, twisting and turning at incredible speeds were screeching like a banshee. The jet was nose diving somewhere just off the coast of Virginia over the Atlantic Ocean.

The g-force was incredible, Bill couldn't hang on much longer, his arms were tired and the pressure was just too much, and he felt himself starting to weaken and become nauseous. He looked to his side at Phil sitting in the co-pilots seat. Phil was white as a sheet. His hands were clutched like vices on the arms of the seat, and he looked as though he were frozen in fear, if not already completely dead from fright. Phil's eyes were wide open, yet there was no sign of life, not so much as a blink or twitch. Even as the rain spitting through the cracked cockpit window sprayed against his face, Phil remained motionless.

"Phil. This is it. We're going to hit and hit hard! We're in God's hands now." Bill shouted.

Bill really couldn't tell if Phil was alive or dead, but he had to say something. He could feel the steering yoke pulling free from his grip, and he could feel they were spinning in a clockwise motion at a 180 degree nose dive. He knew they were off shore. He at least managed to fly them to the shore line knowing full well they would have no chance of survival had they been nose diving into solid land. This way at least there was a small chance they might survive. It was the slightest of chances but it was better than none at all. It was as he had said — *they were now in God's hands.*

Phil wasn't dead but he was frozen in fear. Phil's worst fear among all fears was happening and there was no escaping. His life was flashing through his mind like a slide show being shown in a room filled with strobe lights. Yet there was this repetitive thought that kept playing over and over in the forefront of his mind, *"This can't be happening! "*

What were the chances of a bolt of lightning streaking right through one of the wing engines just as they were about to pass out of the storm? To make matters even more miserable was the fact that they were only about 15 minutes away from clear skies and a smooth flight the rest of the way. It was hardly even conceivable. Yet it happened and now all hell broke loose.

Phil watched as the black, choppy, and angry looking waters of the ocean appeared, he saw Bill out of the peripherals of his sights turn his head back to look straight out the cracking cockpit window. The cockpit window gave way and shattered like dust. They were blind for that fraction of a second just as they hit the ocean, nose first, and were swallowed almost gracefully by the monstrous waves of the Atlantic.

Flares and radar beacons deployed like fireworks from the tail of the plane seconds before they hit. However in less than a minute there wasn't a trace of any of it or even of them. There was nothing left but the mighty roar of the ocean and its angry waves, and the booms of the thunder, and the streaks of lightning in the skies above.

ooooo

Chapter 30

Lusting passion

Quinn slowly eased back onto the bed. He was mentally and emotionally exhausted. He felt like he had just run a 100 mile marathon. His eyes were heavy and he just didn't want to think anymore. His eyes closed and in seconds he was asleep. His heavy breaths were loud as he drifted deeper and deeper into a much needed nap.

Brock and Tonya both looked at Quinn as his half snoring breaths suddenly filled the room. Their eyes moved from Quinn to connect with each others. It was like they could read each others eyes.

"We should... let him rest." Brock whispered.

Tonya nodded and immediately reached for her purse. Brock opened the door and let Tonya out first and followed closely behind her. Once they were out of the room, he closed the door quietly behind them.

"We could just hang out in my room for a little while if you want to?" He asked suggestively and moved to open the door to his room.

Tonya felt a blush creeping up her cheeks. She was tired but she wanted nothing more than to be able to spend some time alone with Brock for the first time this evening.

Brock opened the door to his room and again let Tonya go through first. Tonya entered and set her purse down beside the dresser. Brock entered in the room close behind her and closed the door, and locked it.

"Do you mind if I use your washroom real quick?" Tonya asked in a shy tone.

"Not at all, go ahead." Brock said with a smile.

Tonya had butterflies and her heart was racing. The first thing she did when she went into the washroom was turn the tap on to let the sound of running water trickle out of the faucet. She placed her hands on the sink and leaned her upper body forward slightly and looked herself over in the mirror. She looked a little tired she thought but her makeup was still perfectly intact. She fixed a few loose strands of hair that were out of place and then used the toilet.

Brock in the meantime was fiddling with his iPod trying to hook it up to the TV to get some music playing. It was very quiet in the room and in desperate need of some ambient sound. He flicked through his songs until he found some 'Kravitz'. In a moment the song "Love" started playing.

It was perfect in mood, sound, and timing as Tonya just then entered back into the room. Their eyes locked onto each others again. It was an undeniable wanton look, both raw and passionate. Brock moved slowly to the end of the bed and sat himself down.

Tonya took a few more steps toward the TV and picked up the iPod. Her back was turned to Brock as she thumbed through it.

A small smile curved her lips, "I haven't heard this song for awhile." She said and threw a quick glance over her shoulder at Brock.

Brock was looking at her quietly, admiring her from behind, his eyes roaming down her back taking in every little curvature of her form. He smiled and said, "Mmm... Kravitz is one of my faves."

He raised himself slowly to his feet again. He couldn't resist it any longer. Her neck and shoulders looked so smooth and inviting. He needed to set his hands gently upon them and plant a kiss on her neck.

The butterflies in Tonya's stomach were exploding inside of her as the music played softly in the background and she heard Brock raise himself from the bed. Her body tightened a little.

Tonya sucked in her tummy and arched her lower back inward. Her small perky bottom lifted slightly as she felt Brock move close behind her. Her body tingled and trembled excitedly as she now felt his breath close to her neck and shoulders. An uncontrollable gasp softly escaped her lips as she felt his big, warm hands cup her shoulders, and slowly smooth their way down her arms.

Tonya's body was trembling and she felt like she was melting as Brock's lips kissed the back of her neck. She set the iPod down and gripped the edge of the dresser. It was all she could do to keep herself from collapsing from the sensual bliss she was feeling at that second.

Another un-controllable gasp exploded from Tonya's lips as his hands roamed up and down her sides inching their way to rest on her hips. She could now feel the bulge of his crotch pressing against her bottom. His hands were firmly but sensually gripping her around her hips. His kisses on her neck and shoulders and back were becoming more and more heated and passionate. Her body was giving in quickly to him; she slowly started matching his rhythm pressing back to him.

Her chest was heaving and her breaths were hard and deep.

Brock's breaths were deep and hard also, and he was becoming a little more aggressive. He was guiding her hips so that her bottom was pressing tighter against his crotch as he kept grinding and pressing against it.

Tonya was lost in the heat of passion, their rhythm becoming as one as they bumped and grinded against each other. She could feel how hard he was, and it felt thick and large poking at her. His shorts and her thin dress were the only things separating them from being locked together.

Tonya's body was trembling, and when she felt his mouth start to kiss down between her shoulder blades, her body instinctively leaned forward, allowing him to.

She felt his hands move from her hips to down the outside of her thighs, inching lower and lower until he started pulling up her dress as he moved his hands back up. Just feeling her dress inching up her thighs was making her insides build with anticipation, and excitement. She felt herself dampen between her legs.

Tonya couldn't help her desires and he felt so good pressing up behind her.

Brock's kisses became extremely intense, as he made his way halfway down her back. His hands had her dress hiked up around her hips by now. Her perky bottom arched and exposed.

Tonya could feel his eyes burning as they gazed onto her thong strap that rode up between her cheeks. Then she felt one of his hands move off her hip as he pulled back slightly from her.

She could feel him loosening the button from his shorts, and the sound of his zipper being pulled down. The thud of his shorts hitting the floor, and then feeling him urge her to bend forward a little more made her start dripping.

Tonya bit on the corner of her lip feeling his thumbs hook into the sides of her thong. He was easing them down, not too fast but not too slow either. Her legs started to tremble as she felt her thong slide down to her ankles, she instinctively stepped out of them without breaking the position he had her in.

Then she felt it. His manhood pressed tight against her from behind. It was hot and it felt so smooth and hard. Again she gasped feeling his skin against hers. She arched even more, she couldn't help herself. He started with his rhythm again pressing back and forth, up and down grinding himself against her. She matched his rhythm, and could feel him sliding up and down her; his manhood sliding its way to between her cheeks. It felt thick, and oh so hot, and incredibly smooth.

Tonya's hands gripped the edge of the dresser even tighter as his strokes became longer and harder. She was dripping wet, and so ready to feel him inside of her. She could feel herself getting damp between her cheeks as his manhood kept sliding up and down between them. She was soaked for him. She could feel every inch of his shaft gliding along crack. She never felt anything quite as intense as that before.

Hearing his deep grunting moans and feeling him slide against her like that turned her on even more.

Then she felt one of his hands move up her back until he carefully but firmly entwined a fistful of her hair into his hand. He gently yet firmly tugged on her hair so she would arch her head back.

She did willingly.

Tonya felt him pull back from her slightly as he adjusted himself and at that very moment her body began to tremble as she felt the tip of his manhood press against the entrance of her dripping wet pussy.

Tonya's jaw dropped and her eyes flashed open wide as she felt him pressing inside of her. Brock didn't let up on the pressure, she felt herself taking him inch by inch, gripping him like a glove. His girth was incredible. He was by far the largest she ever had inside of her. Her hand quickly shot down to between her legs and she started pressing and rubbing her clitoris as he pushed himself deep inside her.

They moaned as their rhythm quickly found each other. She was taking him willingly and sensually with every stroke as he pushed in and pulled back, both their moans grew louder with each passing moment until they climaxed at the same time with each other as the music played on in the background.

∞∞∞

Chapter 31

Maria the brave

After what seemed like hours of struggling to reach the key on the end table with her toes, Maria finally managed to grasp the key and get it into her hands. She struggled painfully trying to twist her hands and wrists into position where she could get the key into the cuffs. Her wrists where bruised and scrapped, and bleeding but it paid off. She got the key into the small little hole on the cuffs and turned it until they clicked and released their lock. She immediately pulled her thong that was used as a gag off and tossed it to the other side of the room.

She was free.

Even though it seemed like hours to Maria it was really only about a half hour that had passed since the time she regained consciousness and started trying to get free. She wasn't wasting another second now. She was naked but she didn't care. She was disoriented and didn't know where she was or how to get out of there but she was determined and ready to run for her life.

Maria immediately opened the door from the room, and peeked out into the hallway. She could see that there were stairs that led up to somewhere. There were doors on either side of the small narrow hallway as well.

Maria still had no idea she was on a boat even though the motion of being on water was evident had she had the time to relax and think about it. She crept out of the room and bounded down the small corridor and made it to the stairs. She pounced up those without stopping. When she got to the top of the stairs she whipped her head around looking for the nearest exit. She was in some sort of lavish looking open concept living room and kitchen.

There were only a couple small windows along the sides, and oddly there was no way to open them. They looked like they were sealed.

Maria noticed more stairs at the opposite side of the room that led upward again. A large TV mounted on the wall was on but she didn't notice the content of the images. It was the video of her being raped. It was loud and the sounds of her moans and squeals didn't even, phase her. She wasn't paying attention to that. She was too concentrated on finding a way out.

In a flash she was bounding across that room to the far set of stairs. It was only then when she reached the top of those stairs that she immediately realized she was on a boat. It was pitch black but the little LED-lights all around the boat lit up the bridge area where she was now standing.

Just then Jacob happened to be coming down the cockpit stairs to the bridge and stopped dead in tracks as he neared the bottom of the stairs. He was shocked to see her loose. He quietly reached to the back of his shorts and pulled out his gun and proceeded to aim at her.

Maria's instincts were on full alert and the little hairs on the back of her neck stood on end. She felt like there were eyes on her. She turned her head just slightly to glance behind her, over her shoulder only to catch the quickest of glimpses of Jacob standing just a few feet behind her. She didn't waste a split second before trying to leap toward the side of the boat and jump overboard. As she did, Jacob pulled the trigger and fired 3 shots.

167

Maria made it over the side and dived bravely into the black waters. Her tiny body made only the smallest of splashes. It was a barely noticeable sound.

"SHIT! FUCK!" Jacob shouted as he watched her dive into the ocean. He shook his head and stomped over to the side of the yacht and looked over. His head was darting side to side as he squinted trying to see her. As he leaned over the side a little and then pulled back; he looked down to his shirt and noticed blood was smeared on it. The side of the yacht right where Maria dove over was sprayed with her blood and that meant she was shot at least once.

He aimed his gun at the water and started firing, emptying his clip into the ocean for safe measure hoping he'd shoot her again to finish the job. Either way he knew she wouldn't survive. They were roughly halfway between PDC and Cozumel-there wasn't any chance she could make it to either shore. With that in mind and the fact she was shot-if she didn't die from the wound, or drown-the sharks would get her.

Jacob just shook his head again and swore a few more times before heading back up to the cockpit. He was on his way to Cancun. He received Luke's message and had just finished setting the coordinates to head there before he found Maria on the deck trying to escape. He was just about to go have one more round of fun with her before he dumped her overboard anyways.
Jacob was just pissed off he wouldn't be able to have his last round of fun with her.

"Fucking Bitch!" Jacob shouted as he moved the throttle on the yacht to high gear and roared off into the darkness riding the waves toward Cancun.
Meanwhile in the black cold waters, Maria surfaced.

Maria's eyes watched the lights of the yacht fade quickly as it motored away. Her body felt numb. The water was cold. She tried to move her arms but they wouldn't move. She felt nothing. She thought maybe she just needed to float and rest awhile. She felt tired and was starting to drift off in and out of consciousness.

If it wasn't for the salty water splashing in her mouth causing her to choke she might have drifted off at any moment. She attempted to move her arms and kick her feet again in an effort to swim but nothing was moving. She didn't feel any pain at all and it was strange because she knew how sore she was before she dove into the water. All she could do was look at the sky and hear the sounds of the ocean. She didn't hear the tail fins of sharks splashing not far from her though. She didn't even feel something bump her back from under the dark waters.

Her life was slowly draining from her, from two bullets in her back, and she didn't even know it.

Maria's only thoughts were to get back to shore, to see the love of her life again, and to be in his loving arms; to kiss his lips and to just see him one last time.

But those thoughts ended abruptly as a shark latched onto her leg and dragged her violently beneath the surface of the ocean and deep below into the dark, salty waters.

Maria was gone...

∞∞∞

Chapter 32

Jack updates Harvey Duke

Shot after shot rang out in the night from somewhere out in the waters. It was distant but not all that far from the shore. To an experienced ear the sounds of those gunshots were unmistakable. It made Jack Delaney stop dead in his tracks.

"Quiet!" Jack shouted. All of the cops at the docks hushed their voices to muffles. Shot after shot could be heard. They were perfectly executed shots. One second between each one. He counted at least 9 shots.

Jack walked slowly down one of the docks at the marina and looked out toward the straight. He could see the distant lights of one of the resorts on Cozumel from where he was standing.

"*He's right out there somewhere.*" Jack murmured to himself. "*And I'm just a little too late*" he said with a heavy sigh. He took a deep breath and turned to walk back to the cops on the shore. He looked to the chief and told him to notify the coast guard. He wanted an all points bulletin put out on a large yacht named the 'The Monster's Ball'. He wanted it boarded, searched and anyone found on it was to be apprehended and kept alive, until he could personally interrogate him or them.

The chief tried explaining he didn't have the authority to order the coast guard on a search mission. It would have to come from higher up. Getting the higher up's to agree to it might not have been such a problem, had Phil arrived in PDC.

Jack got into one of the cop cars and dialed the number of Harvey Duke, his employer.

"Harvey. It's Jack here."

"Yeah, hey Jack what's going on?"

"Well I'm close. Problem is I'm going to need some pull. I need the coast guard to track down a yacht for me."

Harvey paused a minute. "You need the coast guard? I don't know Jack. That's a tall order. Let me try and get a hold of Phil, and uh… we'll see what we can do. What all do you have for me so I can brief Phil on what's happening."

Jack took a deep breath before answering. "The guy or guys we're looking for are on a yacht called the monster's ball. The girl was seen being brought onto that boat while she was out cold. There's also a limo driver that might be linked to this somehow which I'm about to go find now." Jack briefed Harvey, and paused for a minute.

"Good work! Is there anything else? Anything you need other than the coast guards?" Harvey asked.

"Here's the situation. I'm so close I can smell this dirty fucker! The problem is… I think it's too late for the girl." Jack explained with an element of irritation in his voice.

"That's not good news Jack. Why do you think that?" Harvey asked.

Jack took a moment. "My gut tells me that. I heard shots somewhere out in the straight between Cozumel and the marina we're at. I'm pretty sure we were just a little too late. Only thing we can do now is catch this guy." He explained.

Harvey was quiet again for a minute. "Phil is not going to be happy about this. Here's what I'm going to do. I'm putting an emergency watch bulletin out to all the docks between Cancun and Punta Allen… how does that sound?"

"That sounds good. Not going to be a hell of a lot I can do now except wait for daylight to break, unless this limo driver who goes by the name of Miguel Sanchez has something more for me, and believe me I'm going to squeeze him hard until he tells me everything."

"Alright Jack you do that. I'll get back to you as soon as I get a hold of Phil." Harvey said and hung up the phone.

Jack slipped his phone back into pocket and got back out of the patrol car. He had the police chief keep a squad at the marina just in case the Monsters Ball returned. He didn't think there was any chance of that happening but if luck were on his side it just might.

Jack was given a couple officers to accompany him to find Miguel Sanchez. One of them actually knew exactly who he was and what limo he drove. It wouldn't take long to track him down. After cruising up and down 5th Ave. and patrolling between a few of the local hot spots, they spotted the limo of Mr. Sanchez. He was parked outside a well known rub and tug. Jack told the cops to stay outside and watch the limo and to arrest Mr. Sanchez if they spotted him. He was going inside to hopefully find him first and spend a few moments of alone time with him.

Jack entered into the dimly lit rub and tug. It smelled of sex and cheap beer. A small sneer formed on his mouth as he approached a short beer bellied man who was leaning back on his chair behind the front desk.

"I'm looking for Miguel Sanchez. He's a limo driver." Jack said in a low tone.

"Ahh Miguel… Si… MIGUEL!!!" The short beer bellied man yelled out.

"Si?" Miguel could be heard calling back.

Jack looked past the front counter down the small corridor behind it and watched to see if a door opened. One door did open.

It was the second door on the left and seen that Miguel peeked his head out. Jack quickly marched past the front counter and down the small corridor toward Miguel. Miguel ducked back inside seeing Jack moving toward him quickly, and slammed the door to the room shut.

Jack was in no mood for playing around. He was pissed off. He knew it was too late for Maria now. Now he just needed to find the people responsible. As he approached the door he paused for a second. He gave it a hard kick, busting it straight open. Splinters of wood went flying everywhere and Miguel who had his body pressed up to the door went flying back a few feet landing hard on his back. He stormed into the room and immediately stood over Miguel. The young girl who was in the room with Miguel wasn't wearing a shirt and went screaming out of the room frightened to death.

"Mr. Sanchez... You and I have some things to talk about!" Jack growled and grabbed him by the throat. He guided him up to his feet and told him to sit on the bed. Jack then pulled out his gun and pressed the barrel to Miguel's temple.

"Give me your phone!" Jack ordered. Just then the short beer bellied man rushed into the room to see what was going on. Jack pointed the gun at him and said... "Back off and go about your business."
The beer bellied man lifted his hands surrendering to Jack immediately and backed off exactly like Jack told him to.

Jack then slammed the barrel back against Miguel's temple–hard. Miguel moaned in pain and lifted his hands. Miguel's temple started to swell and bruise immediately. Miguel was trembling in fear. He didn't know who Jack was or why he wanted his phone, but he would give it to him without hesitation. Miguel reached over to his suit jacket that was draped over the back of a wooden chair, and dug his hand into the inside pocket and pulled his phone out.

"Don't shoot me... whatever you want–Miguel give ok?" Miguel started crying.

"Oh you got that right Mr. Sanchez. You're going to give me EVERYTHING I want!" Jack growled again.

Jack snatched Miguel's phone out of his hand and immediately started searching through it to the recent calls, messages, and photos. It didn't take Jack long to find what he was looking. It was the picture message he sent to Jacob of Brock, Quinn, and Maria. He brought up the picture, and turned the phone so Miguel could see it.

"Who did you send this to? I WANT HIS NAME MOTHER-FUCKER!" Jack screamed loudly. His voice was frightening.

Miguel was trembling so hard he couldn't help that he started urinating down his leg.

"I... I..." Miguel couldn't even talk he was so scared.

Jack cocked the hammer back on the gun. "You got 3 seconds."

"ONE" Jack screamed.

"His... his... name is Jake is all I know senor. He gives me things for pictures of pretty girls and where he can meet them and then he makes movies with them. He gives me the movies so I can watch them after. That's all I know Senor." Miguel blurted out in a panic.

"Where is he now?" Jack asked feeling pleased how easy it was to make Mr. Sanchez cooperate.

"I..." Miguel started saying.

"TWO! MOTHER-FUCKER!" Jack yelled again pressing the gun harder against Miguel's temple.

"I don't know senor... he never meets me. I met him only one time a long time ago. I don't know where he lives. He's an American. He's a big strong man. That's all I know. I swear Senor!" Miguel blurted out everything he knew. He was shaking and crying.

Jack started searching through the phone more and noticed all sorts of messages back and forth between Miguel and this "Jake" guy. It looked like Miguel would send a picture of a girl with a short message saying her whereabouts and then "Jake" at some point would reply back with some sort of letter and numeral combination. It looked like some kind of code.

"What are all these codes for?" Jack asked.

Miguel didn't waste a second replying to Jack this time. "It's for the website he puts the movies on. He gives me the codes and I can watch the movies he made with the girls."

"What's the website?" Jack asked.

"It's uh…uh…" Miguel hesitated.

"THREE" Jack screamed, but was interrupted before he could finish saying 'mother-fucker'.

"It's at xxxthemonstersballxxx.com" Miguel wailed. Miguel was absolutely petrified feeling like he came a mere second away from having a bullet to the brain.

"GET UP!" Jack yelled and grabbed Miguel by the back of the neck and shoved him out of the room and into the hallway. He threw Miguel so hard that he slammed into the wall and slumped to the ground.

Jack grabbed Miguel roughly and lifted him back up to his feet. Jack shoved him down the hallway and kicked him in the ass to keep him moving fast.

The short beer bellied man behind the counter just kept his hands held up high as Miguel and Jack went past. He breathed a huge sigh of relief as they left.

Once outside, the two cops Jack had been riding with got out of the cruiser and grabbed Miguel and quickly cuffed him.

"Book him for Human Trafficking." Jack told them "And put him in the dirtiest cell you have." Jack's heart was pounding. He was so close yet still so far. He still didn't have anything to go on except for now a name, and some information that this had to do with some sort of internet pornography ring. He needed to get to a computer. He was close to uncovering something big—he could feel it.

Jack looked at his own phone again. There was still nothing from Harvey.

"What in the hell is going on Harvey?" Jack questioned under his breath, and then climbed into the back of the cruiser sitting beside Miguel as they drove back to the police station.

∞∞∞∞

Chapter 33

Bearer of bad news

Harvey had attempted to call Phil numerous times. It went directly to Phil's voicemail. He left three messages telling him he needed to speak with him urgently. He checked in with his contacts at all the airports between PDC and Cancun and there was no word of Phil or his jet arriving. He began calling out further. Florida, the keys, etc... still there was nothing.

Phil was hours overdue by now. He should have arrived two hours ago at the very least. Harvey tapped his pen on the desk trying to figure it out what could have happened. Just then a call came in. He was given news that Phil's jet went off the radar about 2 and a half hours ago off the coast of Virginia and had not resurfaced onto any radars. The Jet, the pilot and Mr. Phil Carter were to be presumed dead.

This was unbelievable and shocking news to Harvey. He couldn't even fathom the idea of it. It wasn't processing through his thoughts properly. It took him a good long ten minutes to realize that sometimes odd things happen in life; Things that shouldn't happen but do. It was sad news. The world was definitely going to be a different place without Phil Carter.

Harvey had to give his head a good shake to clear it. The implications of Phil now being gone changed everything. It was Phil's far reaching connections, and deep pockets that made things move and shake quickly. Without Phil behind the helm everything was up in the air. This whole operation was now threatened to come to a screeching halt. Although he was aware this was a family matter. This was for billionaires Brock Castegere, and Quinn Bailey. Deep pockets and cash flow might not be a problem, but without Phil's presence and connections it was going to delay things.

Calling on the favor of the Mexican coast guard now was a virtual impossibility. There were other means available to them however. Where there was money, there was always an alternative.

Harvey dialed jacks phone. It rang a couple of times before Jack answered.

"Jack speaking."

"Jack hey… It's Harvey."

"Yeah I was beginning to wonder what was going on."

"Listen… There's been a tragedy and it's going to change your mission here." Harvey started to explain.

"What are you talking about? What tragedy?" Jack asked curiously.

"Well… Phil Carter. You're employer for this mission. His plane went down on route to get here. He's presumed dead."

Jack's jaw dropped an inch. What were the chances of that happening? "You're kidding me right?" Jack asked thinking it was some sort of weird joke.

"Unfortunately I'm not. This is just devastating. Phil was such a good man. He was a powerful man, who had a long reach with so many if you know what I mean. Now, I'm not sure what all this is going to mean, but it's going to definitely change things. You can forget about the coast guard being called up though. You're going to have to go back and talk to Brock and Quinn, tell them the news. Give them the down and dirty that they're going to have to anti up some money for whatever it is you need to get the job done." Harvey explained

Jack listened carefully. He suddenly felt himself being thrown into the middle of the fire. Now he had to be the bearer of bad news, and ask for money to finish the job. How could he do that now? Knowing full well that Maria was probably already dead? The mission had now changed to finding Maria to finding the ones who did this to bring them to justice.

"Ah come on man. This whole thing is spinning out of control. She's gone. Something went wrong on that boat, I heard the shots out there in ocean and everything in me tells me it's too late. All I can do now is try to find whoever is responsible. So what am I supposed to say to those kids?" Jack asked.

"I don't know but can you just abort? I'd like to see you finish this off Jack." Harvey replied.

Jack let out a big sigh. "Well fuck it. I'm just going to be straight up with them then. I'll leave it up to them, if they want justice or revenge, whatever they'll have to pay for it. I don't like doing it but I can't do this for free. Time they learn that the world is a fucked up place I guess." Jack rambled.

"Ok well it's your call. Let me know if you need anything."

"Oh yeah by the way, I have something for you. This whole thing is about porn. That limo driver I was telling you about. I found out he's been in contact with our guy and has been sending him pictures of these pretty young tourist ladies, and telling him where he would find them for quite a while now. There's a website called "xxxthemonstersballxxx.com" and I guess you enter these codes and you can watch what this guy does to these girls. Can you check that out for me? I'll send you the codes. Our guys name is "Jake" and I got his number. I'll send you that too."

"Gotcha, I'll get on that. I'll get a team of hacks to get in there and find out what they can. Send those codes, and that phone number to me and I'll let you know if anything comes up... Oh and good work by the way." Harvey said before hanging up.

Jack let out another deep sigh and shook his head as he started forwarding all the messages to Harvey's phone from Miguel's phone. He sent him the phone number of "Jake" as well. He looked over at Miguel who was sitting beside him.

"This time you guys messed with the wrong people." Jack said and stared Miguel straight in the eyes.
Miguel looked away. He stared out the back window with a worried look on his face. He didn't say another word.

∞∞∞∞∞

Chapter 34

Luke leaves PDC

April 24th 3:53 am CST

Luke awoke to the sound of his ring tone he sat up quickly from the bed and reached for his phone. It was a message from Jacob.

"The bitch took a swim!"

Luke stood up from the bed and began to reply to the message. "I'm leaving now. I'll find you at the docks in Cancun."

Luke jumped into the shower to wake himself up and freshen up. He got himself dressed, and quickly gathered all his things and was about to leave the room. He stopped at the door and looked over his shoulder. He was being extra cautious. He felt the need to double check the room to make sure he left nothing behind. He just wanted to feel sure. He didn't find anything anywhere. Not under the bed, not under the sheets, not under the pillows. He was satisfied. He left the room feeling completely at ease, carrying his laptop and duffle bag.

Luke walked quietly to the elevator and pressed the button and waited for it to open. It opened right away. It was empty. He stepped inside and pressed the button to take him down to the lobby. Seconds later the elevator doors opened and he stepped out. He made his way directly over to the front check-in desk and asked the concierge to call him a Limousine.

He looked at his watch and it was almost 4:00 am. He then walked across the lobby foyer to the doors, and stepped outside. There were a couple of benches off to the side in which he sat down on one of them and waited for his limo to arrive. As he waited his mind kept going everything. There were many things he could have done tonight, but nothing that couldn't have waited.

Luke could have sent that email to Brock and Quinn. He could have played a dangerous game. It wasn't worth it though. Something told him to hold off. He was glad after receiving that message from Jacob that he listened to his instincts. Had he pressed send he would've been holed up in that room perspiring with anxiety and the millions of thoughts he would have had running through his mind. Luke would have analyzed each and every little move, even down to each word that was said until he was consumed with his paranoia of being caught. As it was now, he could leave with peace of mind.

Luke just had one little loose end to tie up. He needed to speak to Sandra but that wasn't causing him too much concern even though it was nagging away at him, it wasn't all that important.

The limo arrived about 10 minutes later. He quickly walked over and climbed into the back with his bag and laptop. Just as he slammed the door shut, the police cruiser that Jack was hitching a ride with roared in behind the limo. "Cancun" was all that Luke uttered to the limo driver. The limo started to pull away and did a U-turn to head for the highway that would take them to Cancun. Luke saw the cop car as they made the U-turn and smirked as he watched Jack getting out of it.

"Just a little too late I'm afraid." Luke mused to himself watching Jack disappear inside the resort as they drove away. He couldn't keep the smug smirk off his face as the limo twisted and turned down the streets of Playa Del Carmen making its way to the highway.

Jack on the other hand was not smirking at all, nor was he smug. He was feeling quite frustrated. What started off as a simple search and rescue job was now turning into something much larger and more complicated. On top of that he lost some major pull with the death of Phil Carter. Pull that would have made his job move a lot quicker. As it was, he was just a couple of steps behind the bad guy or guys. In addition to that he felt certain he was too late. Every intuition and gut instinct told him that Maria was dead.

Jack was also now finding himself having to be the bearer of bad news. He had to be the one to explain to Brock and Quinn that not only has he not found Maria yet, but that their close 'Uncle' was presumed dead as his plane went down off the coast of Virginia.

None of this was any good. Jack wasn't going to tell them he feared it was too late for Maria. Jack knew if he could catch the culprit(s) that they would at least have that tiny bit of solace in knowing that justice could at least be done. Besides from what he already seen of Quinn and how the boy was dealing with all this. He knew there would be no way on earth that boy could handle hearing news that it might be too late for his fiancé.

The other problem weighing heavy on Jacks mind was that he really didn't have much time to play around being the sympathetic counselor. He needed to tell them the news of their uncle and explain to them that he needed the funds to be able to continue with his job.

Half of him felt like just walking away from the whole sloppy mess this was becoming but the other half wanted so bad to finish it, and to find who was responsible for all of this pain and suffering. All Jack could do now was–try. He was willing to go the extra mile, he just needed to convince Brock and Quinn to believe in him and trust him that he would find Maria and her abductor.

The elevator opened and Jack quickly stepped out of it making his way down to Quinn's room. He took a couple deep breaths to relax before rapping his knuckles on the door.

∞∞∞∞

Chapter 35

The bearer of bad news

Brock and Tonya were cuddled tight under the sheets and covers of his bed. Music was still playing. It was some slow, blues instrumental song at the moment. A couple hours had passed since the Lenny Kravitz song 'Love' started playing, when they first succumbed to their desires for each other. They moved from the dresser to bed and made love to each other several other times, in several other positions.

Both of them were spent and had drifted off to sleep.

The sound of knocking outside the room woke Tonya up. She thought she heard a couple raps at the door, and waited and listened carefully. Only a minute passed before she heard the knocking again. This time she realized it wasn't on the door to their room but it was just outside of it. She stirred quietly and nudged Brock a few times to wake him up. He was breathing heavy. It was a slight degree less than an all out snore.

Brock barely moved. His arm was draped around her hips and holding her tight to him. She nudged him a little harder with her little elbow a few more times before his eyes slowly opened.

"Brock!" she whispered.

"Huh?" he grunted.

"Brock someone is knocking on Quinn's door I think." She whispered a little louder.

It took a moment for Brock to process what was going on. He was still more than half asleep and was a little confused and disoriented.

Then he heard the knocking, followed by Jack's voice.

"Hey guys... wake up! It's Jack."

Brock sat up quickly as reality all came back to him suddenly. Both Brock and Tonya scrambled out from under the sheets almost simultaneously and started fishing around for their clothes. Her thong was on the floor at the end of the bed. Her bra was tangled in the sheets, and her dress was lying on the floor beside the bed. Brock's clothes were all over the room too. They quickly got themselves dressed and tried to make themselves look as decent as possible, before opening the door to greet Jack.

Jack was somewhat surprised to see Brock and Tonya open the door beside Quinn's room. He wasn't surprised they were together and seeing Tonya's hair disheveled and make up smeared with that look on her face like she just had her whole world rocked–Jack wasn't surprised about that at all. He knew from the first few moments he met them that they had a thing for each other. It was more than obvious in so many ways. He was surprised however for just a split second that maybe he had knocked on the wrong room door. Jack forgot they mentioned that Brock's room was next door.

"Hey guys. Uh I need to talk to you. All of you! Is Quinn in the room?" Jack asked. His voice was a little somber and quite serious in tone.

"Yeah... yeah he should be." Brock replied and immediately opened the door to Quinn's room.

Quinn was sleeping exactly in the same position as when Brock and Tonya left the room. He was snoring loudly, and it looked like he hadn't moved a muscle.

The three of them filed into Quinn's room and Brock leaned over Quinn slightly and nudged him gently.

"Hey Quinn, wake up. There's some news." Brock said as he kept nudging Quinn more and more until his eyes finally flickered open.

Quinn had a confused look on his face for a moment or two and then sprang up to a sitting position.

"What... what's going on? Did they find her?" He asked immediately.

Jack was just closing the door behind him as he entered the room and took a deep breath. He looked at them all gravely for just a moment before asking Brock and Tonya to take a seat. He stood with his back against the door and crossed his ankles. He waited until Brock and Tonya sat down on the bed beside Quinn. The three of them were looking at him with eager, hopeful eyes. Jack exhaled deeply.

"Well here's how it is." Jack started to explain. "I haven't found her yet. I'm close. I'm really damn close. I have a lot of information to go on and it's just a matter of time." Jack paused for a minute.

They all looked at each feeling that glimmer of hope rise a little even though the disappointment of not having found her yet lingered like stale air in their lungs.

"There's something I need to tell you guys though." Jack said with that somber tone growing a little more predominate in his voice.

"I hate to be the one to tell you guys, but I guess it's better to hear it from me then from someone who you've never met. You're "Uncle" Phil... There was an accident. His plane went down off the coast of Virginia on his way here. They pretty much have presumed him dead at this point." Jack told them.

Quinn and Brock were thrown completely off guard. They both felt completely stunned by the news. It was surreal. This whole night now seemed like one bad nightmare. Except of course for Brock, there was a little reprieve after his time alone with Tonya.

"How?" Brock choked.

"Why?" Quinn asked not even knowing why he asked that. It just seemed too unbelievable that two people close to his heart were now stolen away from his life.

Jack sighed sympathetically. "Apparently there was a bad storm and, well luck just wasn't on his side."

Brock shook his head with a distant look in his eyes. "I... I just can't believe it."

"This is BULLSHIT!" Quinn shouted and gnarled his teeth.

Tonya didn't know Phil obviously, and so her reaction was that of only a look of sympathy as she looked at the both of them and rubbed Brock's back slowly and comfortingly. She wanted to comfort Quinn as well but didn't want to chance it frustrating him even more. She just remained silent.

Jack gave it a moment for it to sink into them but he didn't want to give it too long. He still needed to talk about something with them. He took another deep breath and changed his tone to a bit more serious now. "You guys have my deepest sympathies, honestly. I feel for you guys. I know that might not sound like much, and I can only imagine what you guys must be feeling right now. You've been dealt some bad shit luck tonight." He paused again just for a moment.

"Listen guys. Time is moving really fast here and we don't really have the privilege of wasting any of it. Sometimes we just have to suck things up quickly and put it away for another time. I promise you, there will be a time for mourning. My main concern is bringing Maria back safe and sound." Jack felt like such a liar saying that. Maria was gone already he was certain of it but he had to lie. He had to catch the one responsible for this. It was the only thing that would make this a half-happy ending.

"Phil was on his way here to help you guys and his death shouldn't be taken in vain. I have to tell you guys, to finish this I'm going to need some big money. Phil was going to take care of all that but now that he's gone. You see where I'm coming from?" Jack explained.

Both Brock and Quinn looked up at Jack. They had the same look of surprise on their face.

"Money" Quinn growled.

Jack could understand how it must have sounded to them and seeing the looks in their eyes, like they were looking at him as if he were trying to play them.

"Guy's listen I need a chopper. I need back-up and I can't do that without money. We need money to get this guy fast! I'm going to tell you some things I've found out. He's on a boat, and he's out in the middle of that black ocean heading for some other port. Now I've already taken steps to have a lot of the ports and docks watched which will cost a fortune in itself, but if we move fast we can catch him before he even touches land again. I need to know how much I can play with here." Jack explained.

"You're going to catch him before this night is over?" Quinn stood up and looked at Jack directly in the eye.

"God willing, yes." Jack replied.

"Then there is no limit!" Quinn said.

"There's just one thing. I'm coming with you from now on."

Jack's eyes didn't even so much as flinch, even though he did not like the idea of Quinn tagging along. It just meant he'd have to watch Quinn's back and that could really interfere with everything.

"Quinn, that's not a good idea. This could be really dangerous." Jack tried to explain.

"Do you think I give a fuck about myself right now? No I'm coming and you'll have more money than you'll ever need." Quinn said with a raised voice.

Jack looked at Quinn sternly for a moment or two, before he nodded his head. "It's your call kid." He said submitting to the idea.

Brock stood up and put his hand on Quinn's shoulder. "Are you sure you want to do this Quinn?" he asked sounding supportive but concerned.

"Never been more, sure of anything in my life!" Quinn exclaimed.

"Let's do it then." Jack said and turned his back to them and opened the door getting ready to leave.

"So... What? Should I just stay here and wait?" Brock asked.

Jack stopped. He was holding the door open and looked back at Brock. He watched Tonya stand up beside Brock and suddenly got an idea. He reached into his pocket and pulled out the phone he confiscated from Miguel Sanchez. He held the phone up and snapped a picture of Tonya. Brock was only half in the frame at most.

"What the hell is that?" Quinn and Brock and even Tonya all asked at once.

"Don't worry. I've got a plan. Brock you stay with her until you hear back from us. Got that?" Jack said in a commanding tone.

"Ok. I'd just like to know what the hell's going on." Brock replied.

"When this is all done and over with, I'll explain everything to you." Jack said before looking at Quinn. "Are you ready?" he asked.

Quinn just nodded and followed Jack out the door all the way to the elevator. Not a word was spoken until the elevator door opened and they stepped inside. When the doors closed Jack and Quinn looked at each other for second in silence. It was like they both had something they wanted to say.

"Why did you take their picture?" Quinn finally asked. Jack nodded as if he expected Quinn to ask him that.

"I didn't take their picture. I took her picture." He replied and held the phone up.

"I'm going to tell you something. Do you know whose phone this is?" He asked.

Quinn just pursed his lips and shook his head. He figured it was Jack's but didn't know and really didn't care.

"It's that limo driver that snapped that picture of you guys." Jack said pausing to see the reaction on Quinn's face. He could see Quinn's face instantly transforming into an angry look.

"That's right. You have every right to be angry Quinn. Mr. Sanchez your limo driver was part of all this. He sent that picture to the guy who took Maria. This whole thing was planned right from the time you got out of that limo." Jack explained to him.

"That FUCKER!" Quinn shouted and slammed his fist against the elevator door.

Jack nodded. He wanted Quinn to let out some frustration. He knew that Quinn needed to let some of that go. He also wanted to see what kind of rage was built up inside him and he liked what he was seeing. He needed to know Quinn was capable of handling his own a little.

"Now you see Quinn. Why I took that girls picture. I'm going to send that to the fucker that took Maria. And he's going to get back to us. And when he does, I'm going to know exactly where that fucker is." Jack started opening up a little about his plan.

Quinn eyes squinted. He wasn't quite sure how Jack planned to do that by just getting a message. "How are you going to do that with just getting a message back?" He asked.

Jack smirked. "You said there's no limit to money right? I'll let you in on a little secret. With money we can do anything. There's guys out there believe it or not who can do some really whacked out shit. They're code freaks and work for the CIA and higher. They have some GPS tracking code program that they somehow embed into the message. It sends a signal to the satellites the second the message hits the guy's phone–the next message he sends or call he makes lights up his position. This is real top level black ops intelligence stuff we're dealing with." Jack explained to Quinn excitedly.

Quinn was surprised to learn that something like that was even possible. He was happy to hear it though. "How long is it going to take?" He asked.

Jack pressed the button to go down to the lobby. "It'll only take a few minutes once we get there. We're going to meet up with my employer. The guy Phil called to hire me. "We'll be there in a 15 minutes at the most. We'll get the code freaks to set up the message for us, and then we'll send it. Then we'll be on that fucker as soon as he sends back or makes a call." Jack sounded pumped and excited.

Jack and Quinn both got off the elevator and walked out toward the police cruiser that was still waiting for Jack in front of the resort. They both got in and Jack had the cops drive them to the embassy where they would meet up with Harvey and the code freaks.

Meanwhile Brock and Tonya went back to Brock's room and snuggled back into bed. They weren't done with exploring their affections with each other just yet. There was still a couple hours of the night left and they weren't about to let that go to waste.

∞∞∞∞

Chapter 36

Luke and Jacob re-united

It was close to 5:00 am when Luke arrived in Cancun. He had the limo driver take him to the Paridisio El Tempo Resort which was located along the Cancun Boulevard strip. He had stayed there a few times before and was familiar with the area, and knew they had a large dock that the Monster's ball would have no problem pulling up to. Also Jacob would know exactly where it was, so they wouldn't have to worry about trying to find each other. As soon as Luke stepped out of the limo and paid the driver in cash. He dialed Jacob's cell rather than sending a message. It rang only 2 times before Jacob answered.

Jacob answered his phone as soon as he seen it was Luke. He was slowly sailing up along the shore no more than 10 miles off the coast line. He was hoping Luke would be in touch, and was relieved to see it was him calling.

"Yeah what's up?" Jacob answered.

"I'm at the Paridisio El Tempo Resort, remember where that is?" Luke asked.

"Yeah of course I remember. Give me about 15 – 20 minutes." Jacob replied.

"Good. See ya soon." Luke said before ending the call. They both hung up, and both had the same feeling of just wanting to hook back up with each other and get out that whole area all together. Something was spooking them. *They could feel it.*

Luke walked right into the resort and wandered through it making his way to the beach area and to the dock. His stride was calm and steady. He didn't like the anxiety he was feeling. Something was bugging him. It might have been the fact that he didn't have time to finish his business with Sandra. It kept nagging at him.

Luke was trying to think of the best way to deal with it. He was conflicted between calling Sandra and messaging her to tell her the deal was off or if he should still go through with it. He really wanted that property. Yet at the same time his bitterness toward her daughter made him want to forget about the whole thing. Something told him it would be better to just leave it. Call her and tell her he was sorry but he wasn't interested anymore. He was leaning more toward doing that. He decided he would wait as long as he could before calling her. Once Jacob got there and they were both back on the boat, and sailing off somewhere out of the whole Riviera area he would call her and tell her the deal was off.

Jacob punched in the coordinates for the Paradisio El Tempo Resort and shifted the yacht into high gear once again. He was getting tired. It was still dark and he hadn't slept a wink as of yet. He was going on 24 hours of sleeplessness and was starting to get grumpy. He was still thinking about how Maria jumped over board. She was the first one to have ever got away.

She didn't exactly get away but there was always that slim chance she might have survived somehow, and he hated not knowing for certain if she was dead or not. Whatever the case she was gone. He was going to pick up Luke and they would be off sailing the high seas to a completely different location. It wouldn't be long now. Another ten or fifteen minutes and they would be a team again.

Luke was pacing up and down the dock getting impatient. He kept looking at his watch. Fifteen minutes had passed since he talked to Jacob and he was still nowhere in sight. He kept gazing out into the ocean hoping to see the familiar lights of the Monsters Ball. He couldn't mistake them for anything. Those lights were like home to him.

Just then as Luke looked up from his watch he could vaguely make out some lights off in the distance maybe a mile or two out to sea directly due east of the dock. He watched and watched as the lights became brighter and larger. He smiled knowing it was Jacob and his yacht. Already he started feeling better and some of the anxiety was quickly fading away now.

Not five minutes later the yacht quietly pulled up along side the dock. Jacob navigated it perfectly as usual.

Luke wasted no time and quickly climbed on board. He walked up to the cockpit and looked at Jacob. Jacob was shifting gears and reversing the engines to back away immediately from the docks as he seen Luke come up beside him.

"It's about fucking time." Luke muttered. He was annoyed it took as long as it did for Jacob to get there.

"Hey fuck you!" Jacob shot back. Jacob was in no mood for any of Luke's bullshit right now.

Luke was just about to say something right back, when Jacob's phone beeped with that same 'incoming media message tone' that rang when he received the last message from Miguel last evening.

Jacob picked up his phone and looked to see who the message was from. "What the fucks he doing sending me shit right now for?" Jacob swore.

"Who?" Luke asked.

"It's our little spotter friend in PDC." Jacob replied and pressed the button to receive the message.

The picture of Tonya and Brock who was half in the frame appeared. "Oooh, now that's one hot looking chick." Jacob groaned.

"Let me see that." Luke said reaching for Jacob's phone. Jacob let him take it so Luke could see for himself.

Luke's eyes widened for a second then slowly narrowed. He was just staring at the picture for a good long minute in silence, studying it closely.

"What?" Jacob asked seeing Luke's narrowed eyes. He could tell by the expression on Luke's face and by his complete silence that something wasn't right.
He knew Luke all too well by now.

Luke's mind was spinning, his heart started pounding and he felt his body begin to perspire as his blood was pumping so fast. He turned the phone so Jacob could look at it again. "That's the fucking bitch I was with tonight! And that asshole in this picture is the guy she took off with, when your little bitches' man came running into the resort crying like a baby." Luke yelled. His tone was riddled with rage and panic all in one.

"You gotta be fucking kidding me?" Jacob choked. It was more than coincidence.

"No I'm not fucking kidding you. AND whoever sent this–is NOT our little spotter friend. I saw that fucking PI or whatever he was, going up to their rooms before I left. They're onto us man. They're fucking onto us." Luke raged. His voice rose louder and louder with every word he spoke.

"Why? Why the fuck would they send us her picture?" Jacob asked, curiously. It was an obvious trap trying to use Tonya as bait but a little too obvious he thought.

"Because they don't know that I'm a part of it!" Luke answered with a growl. "And… look at the background. They are definitely in a fucking room." Luke raged on. Just seeing Tonya in the room with Brock made his stomach go into knots. It infuriated him.
He took a moment.

"They think you'll just fall right into their trap Jacob. They think you're either dumb or an amateur, that's why!–But they obviously have no clue that I'm a part of it." Luke explained.

"I'll tell you what I know. If they have our little friend – we're fucked! We have to assume they know about the yacht." Jacob said as he shifted the gears back to normal to move the yacht forward again. It bumped against the side of the docks. He shut the engine off as soon as it did.

"We gotta ditch!" Jacob said springing out of the driver's seat and shoved passed Luke as he ran down to small set of steps that led down to the bridge.

"Wait a second!" Luke shouted.

Jacob stopped for a moment to listen to Luke.

"Stop and think for a second. Let's figure this out fast. They're trying to bait you out. If you don't respond they're going to know you're onto them. If however you do respond. They will think they have you." Luke quickly analyzed the situation.

"Either way we gotta ditch the yacht and we gotta go– NOW!" Jacob responded.

"Hold on a second. Yeah we have to ditch the yacht. We have to clean it out. All our fucking money is in here. We have to take what we can carry and everything else has to be destroyed." Luke said trying to work out all the details.

"I've just gotta plug in a charge and this baby's rigged to blow already buddy. Let's take what we can and get the fuck outta' here ASAP." Jacob was talking fast as he was in full soldier mode now. His mind and body was reacting quickly to the situation. He knew what needed to be done.

He raced inside the belly of the yacht and started piling brick after brick of bills into two big army bags. He packed a few cartons of ammo clips into one duffle bag and quickly stuffed some clothes into another.

Luke started packing as well. In a matter of 10, 15 minutes at most they were both ready to jump ship.

"Alright rig it. Then send a message back asking... where?" Luke said. Both of their adrenalin levels were soaring. They had never been so close to being caught before. It was an incredible rush to feel so scared.

Jacob climbed into the engine compartment to attach the charges and set the fuses to the intricately designed weave of c4 explosives he had the Monsters Ball rigged with. He didn't need to set a timer because he was a Black-ops soldier boy; a SEAL, and former D-company, cold-hearted killer. He had the explosives rigged, so that all he had to do was dial a number and it would trigger it to go off.

Jacob was trained for this shit, and he loved it. He wasn't going to set a timer and leave it to chance to go off. He wasn't going to let his enemies have the opportunity to try and diffuse it either. No he had a much easier way of dealing with his enemies. He hurried back to the bridge. Luke was already off the yacht waiting for him on the dock with their bags. He hurried down the ladder and jumped onto the dock without looking back. "We ready?" Jacob asked.

"Yeah" Luke confirmed, with a nod.

Jacob then responded to the message he received on his phone. He wrote, "Where is she?" and sent it.

∞∞∞∞∞

Chapter 37

Operation Rescue/Kill

Jack and Quinn were seated inside a Black Huey UH-1N Attack Chopper, along with 4 others. They were suited up in Kevlar vests and the whole swat outfit.

The Pilot and 3 others were ex military mercenaries like Jack. They were trained specifically for this kind of mission. It was a search, rescue, and destroy mission. They were fully armed with silencer equipped assault rifles with infrared scopes, and night vision goggles. The moment they got the word of where their target was they would lift off and begin the raid and complete their mission.

Harvey was standing outside the chopper with another guy who was holding a laptop. The young man standing beside Harvey couldn't have been more than 21 or 22 years old. He was plainly dressed, wearing faded jeans and a plain white t-shirt. His name was Clive and he was what Jack and the whole Secret Intel Community called a code freak. He had embedded the GPS tracking code that Jack told Quinn about earlier in the elevator at the resort, and they were now just waiting to get a return message. The moment they received a return message, it would give them the exact co-ordinates of the phones whereabouts.

It was almost 5:30 am. Almost a whole hour since Jack and Quinn had left the resort and met up with Harvey. When Jack introduced Quinn to Harvey the first words out of Harvey's mouth were his condolences about Phil.

Then it was straight to business. Harvey had Quinn transfer 3 million dollars into an escrow account. The minute the transaction was verified a uniformed guard approached them with a large metal brief case and set it on Harvey's desk. He then handed Harvey a key card to open it and returned to the far side of the room standing behind Harvey.

Harvey opened the case and in it was 3 million dollars cash in banded stacks of $1000 dollar bills. He nodded at Jack for confirmation and Jack nodded back. The guard walked back over to the table and took the case and left the office. Harvey held on to the key card.

The money in the brief case would go to pay for all the expenses and to all the people involved in this operation. $250,000.00 of that would be deposited directly into Jack's personal account. Harvey would get the same cut. The rest would go to pay for the chopper they were going to use, the ammunitions, bonuses for the cops that helped them out earlier and the salaries of the chopper pilot, and three mercenaries, and of course to Clive.

Harvey then introduced them to Clive who was sitting in the leather sofa that was off to one side of the room. Clive was busy clacking away at the keys on his laptop. Clive barely looked up to acknowledge either of them and just lifted his hand and asked for the phone of Mr. Sanchez. Jack handed him the phone. Clive plugged a USB cable that was plugged into the side of his laptop into the bottom of the phone. He downloaded the GPS tracking code into the phone and then unplugged the phone and handed it back to Jack.

"It's all ready now. Let's just try a test message first." Clive spoke in a monotone voice. He took out his phone and sent a message to Mr. Sanchez's phone.

"Now write a new message and send it to my phone." He told Jack.

Jack wrote the word "Test" and sent it to Clive's number.

"Now watch on my screen." Clive said and turned the laptop so Jack and Quinn could see. It was just a black screen. Like a DOS window open. "I'm going to now read your message." He said opening the message on his phone. A message popped up on the black screen of Clive's laptop. In the black window text appeared. It said "Test".

"Oh wow! Cool." Jack snorted.

"Now I'm going to reply to your message and watch what happens when you get it." Clive said pointing at the window with one finger as he pressed the words in his phone with his other hand "Testing back."

Jack looked at the phone as it received the message then back at the black window on the laptop. Co-ordinates suddenly appeared. It was the exact co-ordinates of where they were right now.

"WOW! That's just too scary!" Jack said shaking his head in awe that it worked.

"Okay let's do this." Jack said.

The four of them left Harvey's office and took an elevator up to the rooftop of the building they were in. There was a helipad on the roof and the helicopter waiting for them with the pilot and crew of mercenaries.

Inside the chopper were the extra uniforms and vests for Jack and Quinn to dress into. When they were done suiting up, they got into the chopper and sat down.

"Send the message you want to send to their phone now." Clive said. Jack didn't hesitate he sent the picture of Tonya to Jacob's phone.

That was 15 minutes ago they were just waiting now, just waiting for a reply. Another 5 minutes passed, until finally the phone beeped. Jack looked at the message.

It read, "Where is she now?"

Clive blurted out the co-ordinates of the Paradisio El Tempo, in Cancun. It was done. They locked in the co-ordinates of the resort.

The pilot fired on the engine and the propellers started to turn. Harvey lifted his hand as the wind started to swirl and blow and started stepping back along with Clive.

Jack nodded back to both Harvey and Clive, and looked over at Quinn as the chopper started to lift off the helipad and into the air.

"This is it. We got them!" Jack said in a satisfied and confident tone.

Quinn's heart was pounding. He was excited. He was going to get his Maria back. The feeling of the chopper ascending up into the sky higher made his stomach tighten. Seeing the mercenaries with their assault rifles in hand, and suited up in black Kevlar made him feel like everything was going to be alright.

As the chopper reached a safe altitude the pilot dipped the nose and steered it north following the co-ordinates Clive gave to him. They were on their way to find the Monsters Ball. It was only going to take them maybe 15 minutes at most to get there, and so Jack started explaining to his men and to Quinn how this was all going to go down.

The plan was to fly the chopper right over the top of the Yacht. If there was anyone–except a young lady of course in the open, they were to take the shot to bring him down. Once the chopper was low enough for them to drop into the yacht safely they would do so. The order was to shoot anyone who moved except Maria. It sounded easy enough to all of them. They were all ex-marines and had all been involved in missions much more dangerous and complex than this it seemed. *'It was going to be a piece of cake!'*

Meanwhile...

Back on the rooftop where Harvey and Clive were both left behind, Harvey had already started making calls to the Cancun police branch. He was on the phone with the captain of the branch and explained the situation to him. He wanted them to quietly send a cruiser or two to the resort just to patrol the area, just for safe measure. The captain agreed. That is... he agreed for a price of course. Even when he hung up the phone with Harvey, he finished eating his muffin and drinking his coffee. Then of course he felt the need to have a smoke. Finally about 15 minutes later the captain made the call and had two cruisers dispatched to the resort Harvey mentioned to him.

It was right around the same time that the police captain made the call to dispatch 2 cruisers to the resort, that the chopper with Jack, Quinn, and the band of mercenaries, was chopping through the sky, quickly approaching the dock where the Monster's ball was docked.

The two cruisers that responded to the dispatch were halfway across the city. It would take them at least another 15 minutes to reach the resort.

The choppers propeller blades were loud and choppy as it roared over the dock.

"Is that it?" Quinn shouted, pointing his hand to the yacht. He first spotted it because it was one of those specialty yachts his and Brock's company designed. It was one of them large magnificent looking engine powered yachts that stood out from anything else. At the rear of it was in large bold cursive lettering the name of the yacht, The Monster's Ball.

"That's it. That's our boat!" Jack confirmed, knowing its name from the young drug smuggler he busted at the Playa Del Carmen Marina.

The chopper circled it first. There was no one visible on board. All the mercenaries, including Jack had their guns pointed and ready should anyone come out of the boat. The pilot carefully steered the chopper over top of the yacht and began to descend to a height where Jack and the others could jump safely and easily onto the yacht.

One by one they dropped out of the chopper.

The 3 mercenaries jumped first, then it was Quinn and last to jump was Jack. He wanted to make sure he had Quinn's back at all times. The team quickly filed into the belly of the yacht. Careful and precise they covered each others backs as they entered. Stopping and starting their search with their backs to the walls. Quinn didn't have an assault rifle but he did have a fully loaded 9mm Glock17 squeezed tightly in his hands. Quinn cautiously started to enter the yacht with Jack following no more than a step or two behind him.

The team inside could be heard calling out clear, clear, clear as they quickly burst into each room inside the yacht. It was becoming apparent no one was on the yacht. Then at that moment just as Jack was about to step inside Mr. Sanchez's phone which Jack still had on him beeped with a message. Jack scrambled quickly to take the phone out, and read the message. It was a one word message.

"BOOM"

∞∞∞∞

Chapter 38

The Devil laughs

April 24th 2010 5:56 am

Luke and Jacob scurried quickly down the dock after they sent the message back. They didn't really have a plan of where they were going, except to get off the dock and go somewhere, where they were out of sight. They were weighted down by their bags. They each had one of the large bulky army backpacks on their backs, and were each carrying two duffle bags of belongings in each of their hands.

Jacob took the lead as his big, powerful legs took long fast strides. When he reached the end of the dock he paused for second taking a quick glance around at his surroundings. There was a parking lot not far off to their left, with a few vehicles parked in it. It was only about 300 yards away. He wasted not a second more and hustled quickly toward it.
 Luke was following close behind trying to keep up with Jacob. He was in a half jog trying to keep up with Jacobs pace.

Jacob marched straight to an older 1990's model white Ford Taurus that had visible signs of rusting along the bottom sides of it. He quickly tried opening the driver's side door and as luck would have it the door was unlocked. He quickly pressed the unlock doors button on the inside of the door to open all the other doors in the car. Then he leaned down to press the button that was located just under the steering wheel to open the trunk.

Both Luke and Jacob quickly wiggled their shoulders and arms free from the army bags. They shoved the bags filled with cash into the trunk of the car. Then they threw their duffle bags into the back seat of the car. Jacob climbed into the driver's side and Luke into the passenger's side. Jacob quickly pulled out his Swiss Army pocket knife and hammered into the keyhole of the ignition until it was wedged deeply inside of it. He twisted it forcefully and the car's engine fired up.

They didn't drive away or squeal out of the parking lot. Instead they sat in the car looking out the windows, on the watch for any cops or suspicious people. They had a perfect view of the yacht from where they were parked. They just wanted to see how it was all going to go down. Jacob reached behind his back and pulled out his 9mm Glock 19. He checked the clip. It was a full clip. Then he set it on his lap just in case.

"You should grab one too. There's a couple in that blue duffle bag of mine." He suggested to Luke.

"Good idea." Luke replied and twisted himself around in the seat to get one out of Jacob's blue duffle bag.

Luke twisted himself back around and took a deep breath.

"Check the clip." Jacob said.

Luke checked it and readied it, and held onto it aiming it at the car floor.

Jacob's ears perked up hearing something he hadn't heard in quite some time. It wasn't the kind of sound any average person would have known right off the get go. It was one of those sounds that unless you had been around it often it would make you guess at what it might be. Jacob leaned his head over the steering wheel and was looking upward into the sky. His eyes darted from side to side as he searched the skies.

"What? What are you looking for?" Luke asked as he watched Jacob.

"You hear that?" Jacob asked.

Luke did hear something it was like a very distant wobbling sound and it was getting louder and louder.

Jacob's eyes widened. He spotted the Huey flying in fast. It had it's headlight on and it grew brighter and brighter until it looked like a white beam was coming out of it. The light of Dawn was just starting, so the sky was beginning to fade from a deep purple to a softer shade of blue.

He pointed to it to show Luke.

"There they are." Jacob whispered, watching the chopper pass across the sight of their windshield. They watched it shine its light on the yacht and circled it once before it moved over top of it, and hovered for a moment. Slowly it descended until it was maybe 6 feet above the yachts deck.

"Get my 'nocs outta that bag Luke." Jacob said quickly.

Luke twisted around again and rifled through the bag until he found a small pair of binoculars. It was one of the few things Jacob had kept with him since his SEAL days. They were night vision binoculars and came in very handy for Jacob many times. Luke handed him the binoculars after settling back in the seat again.

"Thanks buddy." Jacob whispered as he raised them to his eyes. He started digging around in his pocket as he watched the chopper drop a few ropes down. He pulled out his phone, and thumbed something quickly.

"What are you doing?" Luke asked. He found himself whispering too, he didn't know why, he just did.

"Just watch and enjoy the show." Jacob whispered back.

One by one Jacob watched them slide down the ropes and jump into the yacht. He counted 5 of them in total. He watched them start to file into the cabin of the yacht one by one again, until he seen the last of the five bodies of the swat team about to enter. The Huey helicopter began to lift higher as the swat team was securing the yacht.

Jacob threw the binoculars over onto Luke's lap and lifted his phone up and pressed send. Right after he sent the message, he lifted the phone to his mouth and spoke into it.

"Auto Dial 9" He spoke very clearly. The phone immediately called a number he had programmed to auto dial.

"Now watch!" He said again. Luke was watching and even though he knew what to expect he never expected it to be like that.

A sound so loud and powerful broke the silent dawn, and a flash so bright, it lit the sky for a quarter mile in every direction. The yacht erupted into flames sending debris flying everywhere. Not just the yacht exploded but it took half the dock down with it, and another nearby boat that was docked there as well. The heli had not lifted to a safe enough distance either. It was caught in the centre of the flames and flying debris of the explosion, causing it to stall and the pilot to panic. It began swirling and spinning out of control and took a nose dive into the ocean.

"HOLY MOTHER OF FUCK!" erupted from Luke's mouth unexpectedly as he jerked back in his seat, and felt his heart nearly rip itself out of his chest. The force of the explosion was shocking. He never would have expected to feel and see that in his lifetime. It was one of them surreal moments that he would never forget.

Jacob busted out into maniacal laughter.

"Hahahahaha..." He felt incredible seeing his work in action. He felt like a proud father looking at his newborn son for the first time.

Luke was still in a state of shock, and slowly looked over at Jacob watching him laugh like a psychopath.

There were no words to be found, rather only a feeling of having crossed the line of reason and into the depths of sheer madness. His ears were ringing, his eyes still half blinded by the explosion and his head was spinning.

He looked around and all at once it hit him. There was burning pieces of wood and metal falling from the sky, all over the place. Car alarms started ringing and beeping everywhere. Even the fire alarm inside the nearby resort started wailing loudly. Everything seemed like it was in slow motion.

Luke felt like he had front row pass to hell.

Jacob then shifted the gear into drive and slowly turned the wheel. He started driving out of the parking lot. His laugh softened into chuckles; deep throaty chuckles as he drove out of the parking lot and rolled down the boulevard heading for the highway.

In minutes the entire area was buzzing with chaos. Two cop cars raced past them heading for the resort. People were shaken and shocked out of their sleep and began pouring outside the resort to see the destruction.

Jacob just kept driving until they merged onto the main road that would lead them to the highway. His chuckles dissipated into silence. He kept driving, and finally looked over at Luke.

"Where to buddy?" Jacob asked in a flat tone. His voice was now devoid of any feeling whatsoever. Jacob then pushed a cassette tape that was sticking half out of the old tape deck in the car. A few seconds passed before music started playing. It was Frank Sinatra,

'Start spreading the news… I'm leaving today…'

Luke sat there quietly just looking out the window — watching as they passed sign after sign. He was listening to the music. It was soothing.

He was thinking…

He was thinking of where Brock lived and worked. He was thinking of where Tonya lived and went to school and slowly a wide evil grin started to spread across his face. Then laughter from deep within soon forced its way up his throat and erupted from his mouth. He turned his head and looked at Jacob.

"Take a guess."

'I want to be a part of it, New York, New York…'

∞∞∞∞

To be continued…

———

∞∞∞∞

Stay tuned for the sequel...

When Angels Smile
(Book Two)

Coming soon, November 2013

∞∞∞∞

TEASER

Introduction to When Angels Smile (Book Two)

Tonya Wells-Marx was in her kitchen in the process of pouring her second cup of coffee when the phone rang.

"Ooh!" she moaned, spilling coffee on her fingers as she leaned over the kitchen counter, straining to look at the caller id on the phone display. *It said Lobby.*

"Hmm" she mumbled. She wasn't expecting anyone. She wondered if she should bother picking it up. The phone kept ringing. It rang four times; one more ring and her voicemail would kick in. Oh why not? She thought to herself and grabbed the cordless phone off its base, and pressed the talk button.

"Yes?" she answered.

"Is this the residence of Tonya Wells-Marx?" a deep male voice echoed from the other end. The sound quality was bad through the speaker phone outside. It sounded distant, and was hard to hear over all the background noise outdoors.

"Yes it is, can I help you?" she replied tucking the cordless phone between her neck and shoulder. Her ear was pressed tight to it as her hands were occupied holding her mug of coffee.

"I have a document for you that you have to sign for." The voice replied.

She lifted the mug of coffee to her mouth and took a quick sip before setting it down on the counter. Then she lifted her arm to clutch the phone in her hand, still holding it to her ear. She stood straight and her eyes narrowed.

"What is it?" she asked. She had no idea what it could be. She wasn't expecting anything from anyone — so she was curious.

"I couldn't tell you. It's in an envelope." The voice on the other end replied.

"Okay, give me a minute. I'll be right down." She replied and pressed the number 9 on the keypad of her phone to let the man into the lobby, before ending the call. She hung the phone back up on the base, and raced down the stairs inside her condo to the ground level — where the door of her condo led into the hallway.

She stopped at the door and peeked through the peep hole waiting for the man to come into view. The chain link lock was still on the hook. The dead bolt and door handle lock were also locked.

Jacob Stanley heard a loud buzz, then a clicking noise. He turned from the speaker phone he was just speaking into, towards the door leading into the lobby of the building. He grabbed the door handle and gave it a tug. It opened. He entered the lobby taking note of the waiting area off to his left. It was decorated with a black leather sofa and two black leather chairs. There was also a glass coffee table centered in front of the sofa and chairs with two matching glass end tables resting beside each of them. There were a couple of magazines placed on the coffee table. On the end tables were brass lamps with frosted glass shades. The room had a clean ultra modern feel to it. On his left was just a concrete wall.

In front of him was a small flight of five stairs that led up into an alcove. He walked up the steps stopping inside the alcove and found that there were two corridors, one on his left and one on his right. There was a metal plaque bolted to the concrete wall facing him inside the alcove that read, "Suites 1 - 5" with an arrow pointing to the left corridor and "Suites 6 – 10" with an arrow pointing to the right.

Jacob didn't need to look at the suite number. He already knew it was number 3. He casually turned and started walking down the hallway on his left until he came to suite number 3. He turned and faced the door, standing in front of it for just a moment, before rapping his knuckles on the door firmly yet gently.

Tonya watched through the peephole as the man dressed in what looked to be like a black dress suit, with a white shirt and black tie came into view. She also noticed he had short dark hair and was wearing dark sun glasses. He was holding a white envelope. She didn't open the door right away. She waited for the knock. Even after watching him knock on the door with three quick taps, tap, tap, tap, she waited a moment before taking a couple silent steps backward, away from the peephole before she stepped forward again.   She pressed her eye back against it. She did that so the light coming through the peephole would look like she just moved up to it.

"Yes?" She responded to the knock on the door.

"Your document ma'am" The man outside her door replied. His voice was very deep, even through the muffle of the thick metal door that stood between them. It sounded much deeper up close then it sounded over the speaker phone.

She twisted the little knob on the dead bolt counter clockwise until it clicked and unlocked. Next she twisted the door knob automatically unlocking it; as she opened the door, the chain lock stretched to its three inches of give, before it tightened up. The door was open just a few inches. She poked her face through the crack.

Jacob stepped back a little and cocked his head to the side and tilted it down to look at her.

"Hi" he said with a broad smile.

Tonya returned a small smile of her own and responded saying "Hello."

She closed the door slightly and unhooked the chain lock. She re-opened the door and slid her body in between it and the door frame.

He towered over her, standing at least 6 feet 3 inches tall. He had a large and strong looking build. Her guess was that he was in his late 20's maybe early 30's. It was hard to tell because he was wearing dark shades, and without seeing his eyes she really couldn't be sure. He had dark hair fashioned in a Caesar style haircut. He was clean shaven, and she could smell the cologne he was wearing, was Aqua Di Gio for men. She knew the scent. She loved that cologne on a man. It reminded her of someone she once knew.

Tonya's eyes roamed over him from head to toe taking notice of everything from the black dress suit he was wearing, to the Gucci belt buckle separating his white button up dress shirt from his black dress pants that fit him loosely, right down to the John Lobb leather designer shoes he was wearing on his size 11 or 12 feet.

"Tonya Wells-Marx?" he asked. His voice again was distinctively deep to her. It rumbled like a bass drum, lending it an authoritative tone, it was smooth, yet a little intimidating.

"That's right." She replied. "What's this all about?" She asked more curious than ever. He was most definitely not just some courier and judging from the way he dressed she thought maybe he was an FBI agent or something.

Jacob looked down at her through his dark shades. She was an extremely attractive woman in her early to mid twenties. She was close to five foot five. She had shiny blond hair pulled back into a tight pony tail that hung a little more than halfway down her back. She had a taut looking athletic figure, and was dressed in comfortable looking white Nike sweatpants, and a half zippered white Nike hooded sweater to match. Beneath that was a simple tight fitting ribbed pink camisole. Her cleavage was enticing and noticeable. She had a great bronze tan. Her eyes were emerald green and she had beautifully shaped lips that were glistening with gloss which Jacob found to be irresistibly sexy. Her voice was both sweet and spicy mixed together.

He shrugged his broad shoulders and said, "For your eyes only Miss." Tonya didn't notice him reach into the inside pocket of his suit coat with his other hand as he handed her the envelope.

She took the envelope in her hands and looked down at it. It was blank. Immediately she noticed how light it felt as if it was empty. She flipped it over quickly. It was blank on the other side too. It wasn't even sealed. It really was just an empty envelope. She knew right away something wasn't right.

The tiny hairs on the back of her neck stood on end and the coldest of chills snaked its way up her spine. Her lungs tightened. Her breath shortened. Her heart seemed to thud as if tar had just filled inside of it. A knot formed in her stomach. She felt sick. The urge to scream began to rise from the pit of her stomach. Her eyes darted upward to look at the tall man standing before her, only to see her own reflection staring back at her through his dark shades. If she had the time to scream, she would have. She even tried.

She knew at that moment that she shouldn't have opened the door...

∞∞∞

∞∞∞∞

To learn more about D.C. Marshall, visit his website at
http://www.FIERCELIKEALION.com.
In addition you can connect directly with DC Marshall on
Twitter @FIERCELIKEALION.

∞∞∞∞